Shrike

ALSO BY C.M. BANSCHBACH

The Dragon Keep Chronicles
Oath of the Outcast
Blood of the Seer

The Drifter Duology
Then Comes A Drifter
A Name Long Buried

Spirits' Valley Duology
Greywolf's Heart
Saber's Pride

Drax Guard: Crew Six
Flashpoint
Faultline
Conduit
Stoneheart

SHRIKE

DRAX GUARD: CREW SIX #5

C.M. BANSCHBACH

Shrike

Copyright © 2025 by C.M. Banschbach

All rights reserved.

ISBN: 979-8-9890651-5-8

Published by Campitor Press

clairembanschbach.com

Cover Design: Emilie Haney @eahcreative

Drax Guard Logo: Morlin Lorenz @thatmoonysky

To Brigitte.

1

Maya

THE BEST THING ABOUT leaving everything you know behind and relocating halfway across the country to get away from the brother who's into absolutely nothing good, is that he's not around to pop up when he needs something.

Until he does.

I left Detroit over a year ago to settle in Dunhare, Oregon. It's a great city, much smaller and cozier than Detroit, with significantly less obvious crime. Though maybe that was just where I was living in Detroit and the "friends" my brother kept.

It's been great. I finally decided to go to school and get the architecture degree I've always dreamed about. I work at a small coffee shop—*The Fox and Ground*—and am really good friends with the half-troll owner Nadire Antilles.

And I don't know what I am with her brother Besim.

Nine months ago, he and his spec ops Drax Guard team had to charge in and save Nadi and me *in* the coffee shop after an elf sorcerer tried to hold us hostage to get to him. After everything settled, Besim texted to check in on me. And then we kept texting. And talking when he came by the *Fox*, sometimes with the rest of his crew, and sometimes alone. At first it seemed to be only when Nadi needed something—that girl and tech don't get along very well. But then sometimes it seemed to be just because.

And it makes my day better every time. And lately my heart's taken to adding a tiny jump any time his name pops up on my screen. Except it's not under his name. He's *Commander Ryder* in my phone because we both love the *Starfall* franchise—movie, TV shows, video games, everything. A few weeks ago, I convinced him to get online and play a short mission with me. And I haven't laughed that hard in awhile.

But that was three weeks ago, right before he and his team left on some mission that he didn't talk about. Now I'm trying to figure out if I *want* to be anything more. Because even as friends, knowing he's somewhere risking his life, and waiting for some text to pop back up reassuring that he's back in town, is really hard.

But moping's never gotten me very far.

I grab the overfull trash bag from under the counter and head out the back door into the alley behind the *Fox*. There's still a scorch mark on the pavement from nine months ago where a trap sprang and circled me in fire. I'd panicked for a second, trying to figure out how to use my fae magic to get free, when Besim had just tackled me out of it.

I skirt around the dark patch, and sling the trash into the dumpster. I'm two steps from the door when a familiar voice sounds.

"Maya."

I freeze, slowly turning to face the owner, trying not to just get angry at the sight of my brother two thousand miles and one Wasteland closer than he should be.

His hands are in artfully faded jeans pockets, light jacket bracing against the chill from the last dregs of autumn that's taken to jumping around corners in the last few days. His hair is cut shorter than I remember it being a year ago, further accentuating the pointed tips to his ears. Like me, he's got the same bright grey band around his irises marking us as half-fae. It stands out sharp and vibrant against dark eyes and black skin.

"What are you doing here, Emmet?" It lashes from me.

He tilts his head back, hurt creasing his angular features. "I can't come visit my sister?"

I cross my arms, trying to smother the defensive spells trying to leap to my fingertips. "Family usually doesn't surprise family in back alleys."

Emmet's eyes narrow. "Family usually doesn't skip town and disappear without a word."

I scoff. "I left a note, and that was over a year ago. Don't pretend like you care anymore."

It felt like we hadn't really cared in the years since Mom and Dad died, and sixteen-year-old me had kept us one step away from Child Protective Services trying to get us into foster care. Parents dying and leaving you with next to nothing is bad enough, but it driving a wedge between siblings might be worse.

"May." He edges closer and I give a step. He only came around to the small apartment when he needed something in the last few years before I moved. The afternoon sunlight angling through the alleyway hits the tattooed lines on the right side of his neck—the open beak of a bird straining upward in full flight looks like it might try to take a bite out of him.

That's the reason I left. The Shrikes are Detroit's—maybe even the entire Allied States'— most notorious criminal gang, dealing high-powered drugs laced with magic, trafficking, embezzling, literally any horrible thing you can think of. And run by one of the cruelest elves you'll ever meet.

"You know why I left. I'm done with your crap." I jab a finger at the tattoo.

"I need your help." He's still soft and brotherly.

"The hell you do." I back up another step, reaching behind me for the door handle, ready to slam it shut in his face like I should have years ago.

"That's no way to talk to your brother," a smooth voice cuts in and an elf rounds the corner. Something close to a whimper breaks, and my back slams into the brick wall under recognition.

Da'mirchen Kostic. The Butcher. Head of the Shrikes, and surviving member of the Kostic clan after the Feds raided the organization fifteen years ago. I know him by vague sight, the stories whispered through the city, and other tales swapped through the clan that I still orbited the fringes of thanks to Emmet.

If he's here, nothing good is coming to Dunhare.

Damir slides hands into the pockets of his perfectly tailored suit pants, and the shirt sleeves rolled up to his elbows expose muscle-corded forearms. An undercut highlights his pointed ears, the longer starkly blond hair neatly combed. Even the shrike tattoo on his neck has a more lethal sharpness to it.

"What..." I try through a parched mouth. "What do you want?"

Damir offers a smile without mirth, and another shiver runs down my arms. "I want my cousin, and I think you can help with some of that."

Confusion chases through the cold. "I don't know your cousin."

If Damir has a cousin, he's probably running some other underground cartel and I'm nowhere near any of that stuff.

"Think again. Dejan Kostic."

I swallow hard. I *do* know his cousin because he's one of Besim's crewmates. I'd been cautious of him after learning he was from Detroit, and then hearing his last name—Kostic. But then he'd been nice enough, if just quiet and abrupt. And why would a gang elf be part of the military and trusted by *Besim* and the others?

"I still don't know him." I'm horrified at myself. Smarting off to the Butcher, even barely above a whisper, is outside even the ballpark of bad ideas.

"They come through here, right? His *teammate* Besim Antilles, whose sister runs this lovely café..."

There's derision over the word, but I'm locked on to the lingering threat at the end. Some sort of fight tremors to life. "Leave her out of this."

Damir's thin smile almost quells it. "I'll spell it out for you, and I don't like repeating myself."

I nod like he's already said his piece.

"Do you have any sort of relationship with any of them?"

I don't dare clarify what he means, and some sort of violent rage roars up like *I* can protect four special forces soldiers in this moment. "No."

He hums. He doesn't believe me. I lurch to the side as Emmet moves. Damir smirks but Emmet looks at me with something like apology as he reaches closer and takes my phone out of my back pocket.

He's never invaded my space like this, and it seems so violating for it to be my *brother* that I can only stare at him in shock. He holds it out.

"Unlock it."

They don't believe me, and I don't have a choice. Shaking fingers tap in the passcode and give him access.

"I don't see any names in here," Emmet says and another lurch cuts through my gut. He's going through my messages and call history. He frowns. "Commander Ryder? Really? You still obsessed with that stupid show?"

I only glare.

"Who's that?" Damir's voice cuts through, smooth and pressuring.

Besim. I'm afraid the answer is splayed all across my face, and I'm hoping there's nothing in the messages that'll give it away. But the last active chat was weeks ago and they're not holding a knife to my throat. Yet.

"A friend from class. He's into the same *Starfall* stuff as me."

"Just a friend?" Emmet arches a brow and it's like looking at Mom. It's another kick in the gut, knowing how much he looks like them and how little he is anymore.

"I'm trying to make a *life* out here, Emmet."

"Then you should have kept quiet." Damir's lazy voice swings my attention back to him. "Not get your name tied to the Antilleses', and not orbit the same area as De'janick."

The coffee shop attack and Drax Guard taking Janvier down definitely made the news months ago. I'd been interviewed as part of it. Guess I was just stupid letting my name get printed alongside Nadi's. The crew's names didn't because Captain Bron Wolfe, Guard Commander, had been the only one to issue a statement.

"I know they're not back yet. But as soon as they're in town, you'll let me know. I'm sure Antilles will come around for his sister. You are going to get as close as you can and get as much information as you can for us. And if you do a good enough job, his sister won't get caught in the crossfire."

He waits for me to nod because that's all I can do, misery quelling the fight. I'm already close, but I can't do that to Besim. To Nadi.

Damir is satisfied and disappears around the corner. Emmet waits a moment more before handing the phone back. "My contact is pinned to the top. Message as soon as they're back."

"Emmet…"

Something softens for a millisecond as he stares back at me. Then his eyes narrow and he's back to the Shrike.

"As soon as you know something." And he's gone.

I'm a trembling mess against the wall, breath bursting in ragged gasps, hands pressed against the brick like it's going to hold me together.

They don't come back and the alley stays empty long enough for me to pull myself mostly together and stumble back inside. Thank the Fates Nadi isn't in yet today. It's only me and a nineteen-year-old college student chatting with a few customers.

I stay in the back, phone clutched in a white-knuckled grip.

I don't know what I am to Besim Antilles. I don't know what I want to be. But I do know that I can't let them get blindsided by any of this whenever they get back from mission.

They've protected me and Nadi before. Maybe they can do it again.

I unlock my phone. I have no idea if he'll answer, and I don't know what I'm going to say on a voicemail for him to check later. I don't know which option I want.

All I know is I can't let him be hurt by me or anyone else. I press call.

2

BESIM

DESERT SUN IS CUT by a light breeze and an awning stretching over the camp table and benches. My laptop is open in front of me, sorting data from a trafficking outpost we took down in the Wastelands five days ago. I'm keeping one eye on it and one eye on my crewmates playing soccer with some of the kids we rescued.

Sergeant Cieran O'Donnell and Specialist Remy Kalama have taken over the broad space in the middle of the medical camp that's been hosting us for about a week. The med staff had some sports equipment that they co-opted to start a friendly game with some of the kids and young teens.

They're half in uniform, grey fatigues and calf-high boots, but both in short-sleeved T-shirts. The season might be about to tip to winter, but afternoons still get warm this far into the southwest Allied States. My own fatigues shirt sleeves are rolled up past my elbows. Cieran's ballcap is backwards as always, and Remy's ident tags swing over his shirt. I think it's them against seven or eight kids, but alliances seem to be shifting and I'm not sure they're actually playing any sort of structured game. It seems more like running around yelling, tackling, and using magic in some sort of vaguely predetermined rules.

Remy's not really using his, but he's a full-fledged warlock—human with innate elemental-based magic—with fire affinity that's been tuned for war over the nine years he's served in the Army and the spec-ops Drax Guard. It's mostly harmless puffs of deep blue sparks if he does, or easy-to-beat holding spells to keep feet from stealing the ball.

There's a few kids from the Mexican refugees this camp is for. Families have come over the border into the sparsely populated southern Allied States to escape whatever trouble's been stirring in Mexico between territories. They'd been hanging on the edges until Cieran coaxed them in with their broken common and his sparse Iberian.

The rescued kids—elves, fae or half-fae, warlocks, and two dragon shifters—had been kidnapped for their magic abilities and were destined to be shuffled around an underground trading ring until we stepped in. I prefer watching them play to sorting through the data that's other houses and buyers and lists of other trafficked kids.

A lot of it will go to our eastern states division, since that's where a lot of the buyers and safe houses are located. Our job is done after we get the all-clear to head back to Dunhare with the kids and our partners in the Bureau of Magical Affairs. Not that we wouldn't jump on the chance to partner with the East Coast Drax teams and scrub the earth clean of a lot more scum, but I'll be glad to head home.

"Mr. Remy!" A small elf runs to the warlock, reaching arms until he swings her up for her to whisper something in his ear. Remy's been the hero after he made animal-shaped pancakes this morning.

A faint sound draws my attention to the agent sitting at the end of the table. Agent Sara Alder of the Bureau of Magical Affairs watches Remy and probably has no idea how wistful she looks. I force a smile away.

"You can probably go join in. They might need someone else," I say.

A blush suffuses the half-elf's features all the way up to her reddish-blonde hair and pointed ears, and she steadfastly looks back at her laptop. We've been technically working together to put together a case and reports for a joint Bureau and Guard task force, but have both been distracted by the game.

"Hey, no colluding," Cieran yells at Remy and his partner while he wrestles a half-fae boy over his shoulder. The boy twists and gets arms around Cieran's neck, and he lets the kid slide around onto his back.

Remy only laughs and keeps holding the elf as they re-enter the game. He's got a four-year-old son at home, and I know Rem misses him. We're still technically radio silent, but Wolfe's passed some updates to families to let them know we should be home in a few days and are basically out of the field.

It's mostly just to Remy's parents, and to my parents and siblings. Cieran's family is here with us and the dragonwalker warrior he's heart-bonded to. But I haven't seen Athina anywhere this morning, and she should be in the thick of it with him. Remy also has someone here if he'd finally just ask, and she's sitting next to me watching him again.

"You sure?" I ask. Sara's not moving any faster than Remy, and we're all ready just to lock them in a room until he asks her out.

Remy's in short sleeves, something he never does around this many strangers and certainly not around women. He's been hiding his warlock tattoos and the magma dragon tattoo on his left arm for years since a powerful fae targeted him and left him with their son. I think I can count on one hand the times I've seen him in short sleeves around *us* in the five years we've been on a crew together.

"He'd like it if you did." Honestly, the signals they're sending each other are flashing neon and impossible to miss.

Sara lets out a sigh and tucks hands in her lap, still watching him. "I know, but I just don't want to move too fast or make him uncomfortable, you know? I'm waiting for him to make the first move."

And that's one of the many reasons we all like her and are going to keep shoving Remy her way until he asks. The biggest one is that she didn't blink and jumped right in to try to save his son three months ago when Blair got kidnapped by the fae ex from hell. Prior to Sara, Remy has never really talked to a woman outside of basic courtesy and always neatly dodged out of any interactions or larger social engagements.

"How long you willing to wait?" My question comes a little wry. We're walking the line between pushing and always ready to protect our brother.

Sara tilts me a glance that's open and understanding. "Awhile."

And I like her a little more.

"I'm *fine*," the grousing voice of our fourth member breaks and Corporal Dejan Kostic comes slowly over with Doctor Tara Novak. Maybe the biggest surprise of the mission a week ago had been learning that our elf used to have a heartbond with the doctor. That was nestled in somewhere with finally cracking open his past life before Dunhare and learning that he had ties to the biggest criminal organization in the northern Allied States before flipping on them and cutting his heartbond with Tara.

After hearing the backstory on Detroit and the Shrike clan, I get why he didn't readily volunteer information.

"Go sit down." Tara sticks to his side. He still looks pretty beat. The traffickers had raided the camp, stole some kids back, and kidnapped Tara. Dejan hitched a ride in their gate circle trying to protect her and the kids, got tortured by traffickers and then his cousin once the Shrike leader showed up to try to collect his head.

Dejan winces as he sits in a camp chair next to our table. He was in pretty bad shape when we got to the Wastelands hideout, but thankfully Tara was able to stabilize him long enough to get him back here to the full medical team and more magic to start healing all the damage. She also managed to regrow their broken heartbond, and the two of them decided to give it another go. He probably still owes her some groveling after being the one to cut their heartbond in a back-alley removal via sorcerer fifteen years ago. But they're here.

Tara sets down a water bottle and package of crackers within his easy reach.

"Oh good, I know how you get without your afternoon snack," I say.

Dejan shoots me a look from a still-blackened eye before his jaw shifts in a faint smirk around fading bruises. "They didn't have apple juice."

I click my tongue and shake my head at Tara. The compact elf just props fists on her hips and tries to hide a smile, though it's shining out of her silver-green eyes.

"Besim, will you make sure he doesn't do anything stupid?" It's been six days around us and she's already got us all pegged.

Dejan and I scoff in tandem. "I haven't been able to do that for five years, Doc. Sorry."

Tara's lips purse and she levels a finger at Dejan. He raises his hands, masking another wince as it pulls at still-healing ribs.

"I hate that cot. I'm not in a hurry to go back," he says. He'd really only been able to get up yesterday.

"You'd better not. I'll be back in a little bit."

"Go save lives." Dejan leans back in the chair, kicking his legs out in front of him. She gives him a fondly exasperated look and leaves. He watches her a little wistfully before turning back to us. "What's going on here? Chaos soccer with the extremely talented, outstanding Remy Kalama?"

Sara chokes beside me and I chuckle. Dejan smirks. It's good to have him back. Three months ago, he got hit by a fae spell, saving Remy from being caught in another nightmare with his ex. It was slowly freezing Dej's heart and locking away any emotions, causing him to check out and lose will and function. He'd been even more stoic than usual, and we'd all missed the sarcasm.

Reconnecting with Tara had also broken the stoneheart, and it's still a relief to hear his acerbic comments even five days later.

"Corporal," Sara finally manages.

"Agent."

I unscrew the cap and pass the water bottle when he tries to reach for it and winces again. He takes it with a huff and a nod.

"How you doing?" I ask.

He watches the game for a few seconds before drinking. "Progressing past straight garbage."

I'd expected some sort of "fine," but he must also still be grateful to not be locked inside himself that he's answering. He's also not cursing because of Sara or the nearby kids—also a good sign. He balances the bottle on the narrow armrest.

"He's still hanging around?" Dejan asks quietly, flicking a glance across the compound to the young male elf lurking in the shade of a building.

I hum an affirmative. Marko was one of the kids we rescued and seems to know something about the Shrikes. He isn't talking much, especially not to authority figures. Elves aren't usually any taller than five-foot-ten, but he looks short and too thin for his age, and probably spent a good portion of his years on the streets. He's been orbiting the area around Cieran or Dejan though, but Cir hasn't been able to get him to join in the game yet.

"He tell Cir anything?"

I shake my head. "Curses almost as much as you, though."

Dejan chuckles softly. "How's it looking out here?" He flicks a finger toward the laptops.

"Still sifting," I reply. "I was able to pull a lot of data from the computers. Alder's found some active and inactive cases we can link to on the Bureau's end." A smirk pulls the corner of my mouth. "And Remy's really good at soccer."

Dejan laughs and immediately braces his ribs. The humor doesn't fade, especially as Alder mutters something about *"men."*

"We're only giving you crap since you're almost part of the family." I lean toward her, the words getting another flush but a real smile.

"Yeah, don't worry. I've got three months to catch up on with Remy," Dejan says.

"And we've got a whole new world with you," I remind him. He scowls but doesn't argue. We're not mad he hid huge chunks of his life from us, but now that he suddenly has a girlfriend...

I don't miss the glance he shoots at the main medical buildings where Tara must be, hand coming to fiddle with the copper-inlaid dampener bracelet on his wrist. Heartbonds allow for connection between two people. They can share emotions, feelings, and always know where the other is. Which can be an issue when someone's as badly hurt as Dejan, hence the heartbond dampener.

Thankfully Tara and her team had some on hand, not knowing what they might need to treat in the camp. Heartbonds aren't incredibly common, and usually couples have dampeners on hand in case of emergency, but sometimes they don't. And sometimes heartbonds activate well away from civilization like Cieran and Athina's did in the Wastelands almost a year ago.

Speaking of, I still don't see her. She was injured in the same frantic twenty-four hours, but with the med team's medical and magic expertise, plus her faster shifter healing, she's been fine. And she's not around.

Maybe the dragonwalker fleet is having a meeting. A buzzing hum from my thigh pocket cuts off asking Dejan if he'd seen her inside. It's starting to get odd. I pull out my phone and frown at something even stranger.

Maya's calling me. We usually only text, and the only time she's called was months ago when we barely knew each other. She also knows I'm still on mission. I think. Not like she was included in the family update. I assumed that Nadi would tell her since my sister doesn't really keep secrets, especially not from friends.

But Maya's never *called* me.

Something hits my gut hard, and I ignore the fact that it feels like concern, and answer. "Hey."

3

Besim

I want to roll my eyes because "hey" is the stupidest way to answer a phone call when she might be in trouble. And because Dejan's watching me with borderline incredulity since I just answered my phone while still inside the mission parameters of minimal to no contact.

"Besim! Oh Fates, you picked up." Maya's voice comes a little cracked from static, interference from the nearby Wastelands.

"Yeah?" I'm not sure if she's upset or not that I answered.

"I just didn't really expect you to, I know you're not back yet, and..." The words start to shake. I brace my elbows on the table, curling a shoulder up toward the phone like I can get some sort of privacy.

"What's wrong?" Because something is. She wouldn't call me unless something's wrong and I don't know what to do with that. Because I really don't know what to do with nine months of texts and laughs and that night we gamed before I left.

"Um..." Another shaky breath. "I just didn't know if I should call you or not, but..."

"Maya."

She sniffs. "I'm sorry. I should have asked if it's okay to call you."

"Yeah, it's fine," I hastily reassure. I suddenly want to share some more details, hear her laugh, see the way her shoulders lift a little and her eyes brighten when she does.

Dejan's still watching me like I've grown horns. Sara's confused. And I ignore them both.

"My brother stopped by the café a few minutes ago," she says quietly. She never really talks about her brother and has the same sort of tight-lipped refusal as Dejan whenever Detroit comes up. "Someone else was with him. An elf."

Unease starts up, prickling down my arms like my stoneskin is ready to jump forward and protect me from an incoming attack.

"They're...they're not good people, and...and they wanted me to tell them when you all are back in Dunhare." She sniffs again. "Um...my brother is part of a gang..."

"Shrikes?" I ask quietly and a faint gasp of surprise is my answer. Dejan goes rigid and gives a sharp whistle. Cieran and Remy immediately break off and come over.

"How did you...?"

"This elf have a name?" I keep my voice gentle even though I'm furious that she might have been threatened or hurt by either her brother or...

"Da'mirchen Kostic."

"Are you okay?" I grit out, and I can almost feel her surprise on the other end.

"I'm okay, Besim," she reassures, but her voice is still laden with something. "I promise."

It doesn't feel okay.

"Is Dejan related...?" She doesn't finish.

I look up at my team. Cieran's arms are crossed, and Remy's hands are loose by his sides, ready to jump to action if he needs.

"Yeah," I say.

"Oh Fates." I'm afraid to interpret her breathless words, not wanting her to suddenly be afraid of Dejan. Because even if he is related to two of the worst criminals in the States, he's not like them at all.

"What are you supposed to tell them?" I ask.

"Just when you are back in town. And he threatened Nadi if I don't, and..."

"Breathe, it's okay."

She obeys, and another sniff jars the connection. "I'm so sorry, Bes. I just didn't know what to do, and I couldn't..."

"It's okay." I don't really have anything else to say because I'm still spinning on the outer edges of that whirlpool that was going to be fury if she was hurt.

"It's not, and you know it," she returns quietly.

"Look, I'll..." Suddenly start thinking through things because who knows if they're with her and making her do this. Even if she's truly sincere, she still doesn't need information that could lead to her getting hurt. "I'll reach out when I can."

"Okay." Trust fringes her voice, and it brings a different sort of edge. Fear that something is coming, and I might not be able to help shield her from it. If she'd even want me to. "Be careful."

"Let me know if they come around again," I say like I can do anything from almost a thousand miles away. Although maybe Wolfe can get someone to shadow her as a protective detail.

"I will."

There's a pause and I have no idea how to end this call. She doesn't either the way she lingers too.

"I'm really sorry," she finally says. *Sorry* like damage has already been done and I'll be angry, and it'll end whatever friendship we have.

"It's okay. See you soon." And I hang up before I can overthink anything else.

"Care to share, Bes?" Cieran drawls when I take a little extra time setting the phone down and needlessly square it up to the laptop edge.

"That was Maya."

Slightly confused stares are my reply.

"Coffee shop Maya?" Cieran clarifies, and I nod. We've all been around the *Fox and Ground*, so we know everyone who works there, and some of the regulars. It's habit, and my family probably doesn't know that they have a few rough-around-the-edges earthly guardian angels.

Remy tilts his head. "Why does Maya have your number?"

I don't like the scrutiny and the way this line of questioning is going to go, especially since we'll have some big issues once I get to the reason she called.

"From calling me when everything went down with Janvier at Nadi's place."

Cieran snaps his fingers and points at Remy, hopping onto the interrogation train. "Yeah, but why does she *still* have it?"

I clear my throat. "We text sometimes." Weekly, if not sometimes daily. Which I'm fully aware is not something that "just friends" do.

"*Interesting.*" Remy gives me a pointed, and somewhat aggrieved, look. I feel a little more hypocritical for giving him crap and ignoring what's in front of my face.

I swat Dejan's hand away from where he's trying to surreptitiously grab my phone. They all know my passcode and it'll be game over when they see just how much we keep in contact.

"We do actually have a problem," I say.

"We're gonna circle back to the Maya thing," Cieran warns with a faint smirk and his eyes flick to the side like he's expecting someone there. A faint crease around his eyes marks the disappointment at the Athina-shaped emptiness.

"Where's—?" Dejan also notices but his question is cut off by Remy's slight shake of the head and wordless *don't*. So Rem's already asked and the answer wasn't great.

Cieran glares and I start talking.

"Shit." Dejan leans forward, hands scrubbing against each other when I finish.

"She's okay?" Sara asks, and I'd almost forgotten she was there. But the same question echoes in Remy's and Cir's faces.

"Yeah. I think so. I don't think they—"

Dejan abruptly hauls himself to his feet, cutting me off.

"Dej," I start but he pivots, launching a growling stream of Vinland elvish, bruised face twisting in anger and, if I didn't know him better, a little bit of fear.

Cieran cuts him off in the same Slavic-based dialect. Dejan snaps back, but Cir doesn't back down. Rem and I just exchange a glance and a shrug. The only elvish we really know is the colorful words Dejan and Cieran frequently pepper their speech with. A glance at Sara shows she understands and kind of wishes she doesn't.

"Dejan," Cieran says sharply, and the elf subsides. He doesn't sit back down, and stands like he's bracing against us.

"Dej, it's not—"

"My fault?" he cuts me off. "That's my *firren* cousin, Bes."

"And you're not *them*."

Dejan doesn't say anything, just shoves hands in his pockets and glares. Which is sometimes his normal look, or he's about to be extra mulish about something.

"Okay, what did she say they were wanting?" Cieran turns it back to me.

"Just to let them know when we rolled back into Dunhare." I tip the laptop closed. That project's about to be put on hold or transferred to a different team to finish up.

"He might think I'm dead." Dejan's voice is still tight. "I probably looked it."

This time Remy moves, arms crossing and hands pressing flat against his sides. At least he's not acting guilty anymore, somehow taking responsibility for Dejan saving his life months ago.

"But he doesn't have my head as a trophy." Bitterness still clouds around Dejan. "And if he can't get me, anyone I look close to will work for the same revenge."

Remy and I both take offense at the "*look close to*".

"That's the Kostic way." He backs up another step like he's about to turn and run. Something he's never done as long as I've known him.

"Hey," Remy says sharply and Dejan narrows his eyes back. They've been close ever since literally punching it out on one of our first missions as a team, and if I can't get through to the elf, Remy always can.

"That's not you." Remy repeats the same thing I told Dejan moments ago, but the elf backs another step in refusal.

"You don't know me, Remy." He almost sneers and retreats a step further. I watch him regress back to the Dejan Kostic I first met five years ago and if he's not careful, I will intervene.

"Yeah? What the hell have the last five years been?" Remy's arms swing free, and he narrows the space between them. It takes a lot to tick Remy off, and I've never seen Dejan do it this quickly. It also takes quite a bit to annoy me since I have seven siblings and have a built-up immunity to that sort of thing, but I'm about to hold Dejan so Remy can hug him.

Dejan gathers a breath and Remy narrows his eyes. "You want me to hug you? I'll hug you."

Dejan slams his mouth shut and he's suddenly hiding a reluctant smirk because *physical touch* is his worst nightmare.

Cieran just shakes his head, some weary resignation there. In some ways, he's still figuring us out, having only been our sergeant for the last year. But I knew his old team, and we'd have some stiff competition with them in the muleheadedness department.

"Try. I'll punch you." But there's only mock offense there. Dejan still scowls but his stance relaxes.

"Don't pull your stitches while trying." Remy's mouth quirks. Dejan's shoulders sweep down to truly relaxed, and he darts a look of apology to me. I tip my head in acknowledgment.

That's our relationship, existing in quiet beside each other. I know when he needs something because he'll just suddenly appear beside me, and I'll wait him out until he starts talking. He'll tolerate the "therapy voice" they say I have a lot more than he admits to.

"You sure you want to join the family?" I look at Sara, and she just chuckles, only a little red at the comment and the way the rest of them smile. Even Remy doesn't look awkward about it, just giving her a faint smile that she returns. Honestly, these two...

"Go sit back down." Cieran points at the chair and doesn't break his stare until Dejan begrudgingly complies, muttering the whole way. Cieran replies in elvish, and another almost smirk appears on Dej's face. It's smothered by the wince and relief to be sitting again.

"They find her from the attack nine months ago?" Cieran asks.

"That makes the most sense. It definitely made news," I say.

"We think he read Tare's mind. Probably got names from there and made the connection." Dejan shifts to grab the water bottle again and the plastic crunches between his hands. "How many Antilleses are there in Dunhare?"

"Ten," I reply wryly. Aunts, uncles, grandparents are over in Portland or smaller towns around Oregon.

"What's he wanting?" Cieran asks Dejan.

The elf leans on his knees, bottle twisting around and around in his hands. "I think murder is actually pretty low on the list." His face slants into serious lines. "Everything I turned over to the Feds pretty well gutted the organization, plus landed my dad in prison. I'm not really sure how Damir weaseled his way out. I also took a pretty good chunk of change on my way out of town." This time a faint smile breaks and fades just as fast.

"The traffickers indicated I've got a pretty high price on my head and..." He pauses before pointing at his face. "And this is going to look tame compared to what'll happen if he catches up."

"Figured." Cieran settles his feet a little wider. "What about Novak?"

Dejan goes still. For years it's just been him. He's been part of our families, part of our small unit. And he's protected us as much as we've protected him, but now he's got someone else.

"He won't know the heartbond is back," he finally says. "But if he thinks about coming after her again…"

"He won't get to her," Remy promises in a low voice, barely beating Cieran and me to the same thing.

A tight smile barely cracks Dejan's face, but there's some motion to him now, practically vibrating with suppressed anger. I reach out and bump his shoulder and the look he gives me over his shoulder is grateful.

"Even if he doesn't know you're alive, you think he'd still come back here?" Cieran asks. "Novak said Damir had been planning to use her as leverage against her dad."

The plastic bottle crunches in Dejan's hands. "I don't know," he finally admits. "But attacking a medical aid camp and kidnapping a well-known doctor is the sort of thing that definitely gets you prison time, so he might at least think twice."

Cieran nods, glancing at the nearest wire fence like he's planning to defend the compound.

"I'll call Wolfe and update," he says. "He's already contacted the FBI and passed on the after-action reports. I have a feeling we'll be rolling out earlier than planned. What's your status?" he asks Dejan.

"Try and stop me from going," Dejan replies.

Cir extends a fist and gets a tap back. "Tara might need to come with us, and I'll make sure we get a squad or two out here for some extra protection for the camp."

We're all poised to move before his next words make it out. "Get ready to gear up and move out."

4

DEJAN

REMY STICKS WITH ME as I make my way back inside. Having to move this slow is frustrating, but I also know that I would be dead without Tara. The blood loss would have gotten me long before the stoneheart-induced coma might have.

But there's a max limit for healing magic that a body can take before it starts to turn on itself. So since I woke up five days ago, it's been a mix of regulated healing magic and letting my body recover at its own pace. Which wasn't a problem until the news that my cousin is already in Dunhare and plotting to go after anyone I care about that he can find. I thought we might have more time.

Remy's shoulder nudges mine as I weave sideways. I flick a glance at him. He doesn't say anything, and I feel a little guilty for the way I snapped earlier. He's right. He and Bes have been there for me for years, even when I've been a grade A *shilsa*. They didn't run when I spilled my backstory and confessed to being the son of a crime lord.

Just casual conversations between friends.

"Sorry," I say.

His brow arches and his attention doesn't falter from our path. "An apology? Do I make a note for the records?"

I jam an elbow into his ribs and he huffs a laugh.

"Careful. I might even admit you were right," I say.

"Are you trying to kill me?" His easy grin flashes and it's such a *firren* relief to see it after three months of him keeping his distance and looking guilty for something completely out of his control.

"I just..." I start, but he bumps my arm again.

"I get it."

We make it to the med center door and he pushes it open, keeping one eye on me as I navigate the small step up, feeling closer to a hundred and ninety years old than forty-five.

"Still haven't asked her out?" I ask.

His arm slings around my shoulders and I smirk, tapping my elbow into his side again and ducking out from under his loose hold.

"What's wrong?" Tara hurries over from the surgical corner. A few more refugees from over the Mexico–A.S. border showed up last night and some needed medical attention.

"Just assuming something's wrong?" I ask.

She props hands on her hips and I allow a tip of my head. It's been six days and she's proving she still knows me. Remy taps my shoulder and gives us some space.

"What's wrong?" Her voice falls, and concern tightens around her eyes.

I don't want to tell her, don't want to add to the things already keeping her up at night—I know because of the heartbond linking us. Even with the dampeners, some muted impressions sneak through. That and I'm a light sleeper, so I know when she comes in and out of the building.

But I am the poster elf for keeping information from a loved one and that going terribly wrong. So I tell her, and softly apologize when her face pales and she extends a shaky hand. I take it and tug her a little closer. She's always been my exception to the "no touching" thing.

"What does this mean then?" she asks.

"Means that we'll probably be rolling out in a few hours, and you might be going to a safe house." I hate myself a little as she rocks on her feet, eyes widening at the possibility of her entire life being upended—again—because of me.

"Sure you don't want to cut ties with me?" I ask, more than half serious. Letting the heartbond renew had seemed like a good idea five days ago. Had still been a good idea in the intervening time as we got to know each other again and the new versions of ourselves we've built over the last fifteen years. But now?

"Don't you dare suggest that, Dej." Even the dampeners we're wearing can't block the full rush of her stubborn rejection of my words.

"I've been more bad news than good, Tare."

She sets a hand on my wrist before sliding to hold my hand instead of me holding her.

"Would this have happened eventually? Him coming back?" she asks.

I finally admit that, yes, it would have.

"And it hasn't been all bad." She shoots me a look that has my heart beating a lot faster. The way her fingers tighten around mine tells me she feels it.

Heartbonds between elves are as good as a marriage, but it's only been five days. Like before, I'm not ready to just jump headfirst into essentially married life without spending a lot more time together. There's a little too much water under the bridge for us to just pick up from life before I hired a sorcerer to remove the heartbond. Besides, I have no desire to go back to who I was in Detroit.

"Together?" Tara asks.

A poor excuse for a laugh escapes. "I don't want you anywhere near this, Tare."

"I know." She steps closer. "Just tell me what you need me to do."

My forehead tips against hers. "Stay safe." It's the obvious, but it's still my highest priority for her. "Cieran's calling our CO now, and we'll have orders soon."

Her hand on my cheek tilts my head up to look her fully in the eyes and the barely hidden fear of the coming unknown. "Okay."

Like the others, she's not flinching from me and the mess I've brought to their doors. And I fall a little more in love with her again.

An hour later, we're in the back of an Army truck brought by the backup squad a few days ago. We've got an eight-hour drive ahead of us to the nearest Army base. Then we'll take a portal gate back to the Dunhare base, cutting the need to drive almost twenty-four hours.

And with every jolt and shudder transported from the ragged roads to the narrow benches, I'm regretting my gritted determination to come. Even after another dose of magic and meds before we left, and with my own healing magic to ease some of the soreness and still-healing *everything*, this is going to be a long trip.

Remy's next to me, Bes and Cir across from us. They're in full kit—chain mail shirts and armored tac vests over, weapons lying on the floor or propped next to them. I'm not quite up to the weight of armor, so mine is with my pack under the bench. But I've still got a knife belted to my right thigh, one on my left hip, and another in my boot. My bow and short sword are in reach, but it's gonna be another few days before my shoulder and ribs tolerate the draw weight on the carbon fiber bow.

Tara's still at the camp, but she'll be coming later after we more firmly assess the threat. I didn't want to leave her behind, but it wasn't my call. In the end, she might be safer over a thousand miles away.

We also have a stowaway in the corner, hiding behind a pretty clever cloaking spell that Remy could dismantle with a snap of his fingers, but we're all pretending not to notice. I'd never learned how to do that with my magic, instead focused on some attack spells growing up, and then later healing when I became a paramedic. The young elf has been shadowing me or Cieran for the last few days, and I'm not surprised that he took his chance to skip out before social workers could intervene. Marko doesn't seem like he has anyone.

"We gonna talk about it?" Remy asks over the road noise.

"What?" Cir brings his head forward from where he'd been resting against the wall. A shimmer in the corner marks alarm, but we're all still not looking.

Not having the oppressive stoneheart trying to kill me has put me back in step with Remy, and I'm the follow-up for his question. "Athina or Maya?"

And Besim looks so uncomfortable that I can't help but laugh. He's always the confident one, unflappable. And seeing him like this, over a woman no less, is adding *decades* to my two-hundred-year lifespan.

Remy and I bump fists, but Cieran doesn't look quite as amused. His heartbond dampener is back on and he doesn't move to spin it like he does any time Athina comes up. Besim is a bloodhound when it comes to sensing any sort of issue or emotional distress and he neatly takes the opportunity to deflect from himself.

"What's going on, Cir?"

Cieran scowls at all of us. "Nothing."

Besim hums, and it's always nice to not be on the receiving end of that gentle *I don't* firren *believe you*. Except he doesn't curse.

"As someone with a heartbond and the expertise," I start, smirk mirrored in their faces, especially as Cieran rolls his eyes and flips me off.

Even without a heartbond, Cieran and Athina would have been in step. And maybe it's because they only see each other in person every few months so when she's here, they're always together—but it's eerie to see him without her.

"It's..." His fingers sweep toward the dampener and curl back into his palm. "We're having the 'it's been a year, so what's the next step' conversation. And it's going about as well as it looks," he finishes wryly.

"So what's the next step?" Besim asks.

Cieran practically squirms under the question, but answers. "She's ready to discharge from the fleets, move to Dunhare, and plan a wedding."

"*And?*" We all stare at him.

"And I'm saying that it's not fair to expect her to completely uproot her life and move here for me without us at least talking about me going there first." Cieran stacks his fists atop each other, gaze trained on the floor. "She worked just as hard to get where she is in the fleets, and she has family on the islands, and I've got..." He cuts himself off before he can say "nothing."

He shakes his head, tapping his fists together. "I don't mean..."

"We know," Besim answers for us. Didn't mean to discount us, but he lost his old crew almost two years ago, and it's coming up on one year that his sister—his last remaining blood family—died. And hell, it took me a few years to fully trust the two idiots who know me best, so I get it.

"And...I don't know..." He sighs. "I just got caught off guard when she started talking like it was done, and we could talk about literally anything else now." A faint, but very hinting, smile tugs his mouth.

As one, we turn to Besim, and his fidgeting makes it worth it. He's barely the oldest of us four at twenty-nine. Even though I'm forty-five by elf standards, against humans I'm somewhere in the twenty-seven range. Sometimes twelve, the way Remy and I stand in for the annoying siblings.

Shit mode is activating in both of us, I can feel it. And after three months of literally feeling nothing, they're going to be fed up with me before this truck ride is over.

"As someone who has experience with avoiding obvious feelings," Remy starts, and Besim just shakes his head in rueful disappointment as the three of us laugh.

"Spill," Cieran says.

"There's nothing *to* spill." Besim shrugs. "We've texted, and we talk when I stop by the *Fox*, we gamed the other night, and—"

"Hold up." Remy extends a hand. "You gamed with someone not a sibling?"

"Yeah, because you two are useless," Bes replies. We are. I don't like video games and Remy's magic usually causes electronics to go haywire really easily, but that's beside the point. "But I don't really know what that makes us besides friends?"

"I vote that I'm no longer the oblivious one." Remy raises his arm.

"Second." I lift mine and Besim reaches his unfairly long leg out to kick my shin while barely moving. "Ow," I retort and he returns a flat look.

"And she called you to warn you," Cieran says, trailing off without the obvious conclusion.

"It could have been for Dejan," Besim weakly protests.

I snort. "Yeah, she and I don't avoid each other because turns out we're dodging the same criminal organization." I didn't miss the way she glanced at the right side of my neck the first time she heard I was from Detroit.

"You could smile more." Remy turns to me.

"Then people would talk to me." The same face that dared combative patients on late night shifts as a paramedic works really well for normal people to leave me alone.

"The horrors will never cease," Besim says, and a faint shimmer hits the corner again along with something really like a snicker. But we don't notice if it is.

Cieran leans back against the wall again, turning his ballcap forward to make the position more comfortable. He looks to me. "So what's the betting pool like on which one of them asks their girl out first?"

I smirk. "I don't know, is it separate from the 'when is Remy going to ask' pot?" I get shoved over and laughingly curse my way back up, waving away Remy's half-panicked apology because he forgot I'm still kind of held together by stitches and magic right now.

"I'm okay," I reassure when they all look at me. I send the same through the muted heartbond, calming the quick burst of alarm from Tara. There's a bit of exasperation back from her and my phone buzzes in my pocket a moment later. I'll text her back in a bit. I slouch more on the bench, trying to take some pressure off my ribs. Then just end up leaning on Remy when he nudges me again.

Cieran crosses his arms over his chest, eyes sliding closed. He's settling in, and the rest of us do the same. We've still got seven hours and a portal and I'm definitely already regretting pushing to come.

5

BESIM

A CRACKLE AND FLASH of lights marks us driving through the portal gate. Dejan's arms brace across his stomach and he's too pale. But he's still awake and alert even after eight hours. The driver knocks against the barrier between the front seats and the back cargo area. We're clear of the base's gate-port and he'll stop off where Cieran asked him to awhile ago.

Brakes squeak and we shift to a halt. Remy glances at Cieran and our sergeant gives a little nod. Remy snaps his fingers and reveals the elf hiding in the truck corner, bulging backpack clutched to his chest. He stiffens in alarm, but none of us make a move.

"Headed out, Marko?" Cieran asks like it's Saturday evening and beers among friends.

The kid just glares. He's all elbows and angles, ripped clothes hanging loose on his thin frame, and a look that dares us to try anything.

"We're by the front gates. They'll let you out unless you've got somewhere else you want to stay."

"Don't want anything from you, Bluejay." Marko sneers, but Cieran just offers a faint smile and opens up the back of the truck.

"Still not a cop."

Marko shifts to his feet, still holding the backpack. It's full of stolen supplies from the camp kitchens on top of the change of clothes and toiletries the staff gave him. He keeps an eye on all of us as he inches between the benches.

"Keep those ears out of trouble," Dejan tells him.

"You shoulda steered clear of the Shrikes," Marko says.

Dejan offers a mirthless smile. "I am one, kid."

"No, you're not." Marko hops down from the back, leaving Dejan quiet behind him.

"Hey." Cieran tugs a folded piece of paper from one of the front pockets on his tac vest. Marko pauses. "This is my number and my address if you ever need anything. There's also another name and address on there. It's a safe place to go. You just tell them Cieran sent you and they'll give you a place to stay."

Marko slings his backpack on and doesn't take it. "Yeah, a jail cell?"

Cieran smiles. "My last set of foster parents."

The elf studies him for a moment, then takes it, fingers closing around it. "Maybe I'll just lose it."

Cieran shrugs. "Do whatever you want. But I'll be around if you need anything."

"Sure." Marko scoffs, but the paper goes in his pocket before he backs away and bolts for the base entrance. No one stops him. Cieran texted ahead once back in safe cell signal range and the guards won't panic at the sight of a scrawny elf booking it out of the base.

A soldier in Drax grey steps up to the back of the truck, the fading light hitting his eyes and flashing them yellow-red for a moment. The captain's aide is a mountain cougar shifter, generally as quiet and unruffled as one in his human form. Until he eats something sweet and then he turns into the hyperactive twenty-four-year-old he should be.

"Eckhart," Cieran greets him as we disembark. Dejan is last and slowest.

"Sergeant," Eckhart replies easily. When there's no sugar involved, it's a running competition in the Guard to see who can get the drop on, or even startle, Eckhart. Mountain cougar instincts give him a wildly unfair advantage. "Wolfe wants all four of you in his office."

"We in trouble?" Cieran smirks.

A faint smile barely disturbs Eckhart's tanned features. "Not yet, but I wouldn't put it past you to find something between here and the office."

"Hurtful, but true." Cieran taps Eckhart's shoulder. "Lead the way."

"Absolutely not." Eckhart steps aside to walk alongside Cieran. We chuckle. He's learned well.

I take Dejan's weapons, and Remy shoulders his pack. Dejan makes a token protest, but we just point him to follow the others. We take it slow up the steps into the main entry of the Guard tower.

Dejan's arm presses toward his stomach by the time we make it in, but he shakes his head in response to Cieran's wordless offer of support.

We cross the mosaiced fire drake wrapped around a sword and our logo *Fear No Fire* underneath. The memorial wall rises to our left, and Cieran glances its way. It's one of the first times I've seen him acknowledge it since his old team's names and pictures went on it a little over two years ago.

Stairs up to the fourth-floor office are out of the question for Dejan, so we fit ourselves into the elevator. Dejan leans back against the wall. Cieran shakes his head, grabbing the pack from Remy and jerking his head at the elf.

The warlock leaves Dejan no choice as the doors swing open, and slings an arm around him.

"It's *firren* fifty feet," Dejan immediately complains.

"Stop being a martyr or Besim's going to carry you," Remy retorts.

I lean closer and Dejan gives me one of his best glares. He doesn't pull away from Remy, and keeps his arm propped on the warlock's shoulder as we make our way down the hall to Wolfe's office.

Eckhart keeps one eye over his shoulder as he opens the door. Captain Bron Wolfe stands behind his heavy oaken desk as we file in. He's human, and the only magic he has is a glare that can cut stone.

"I thought I heard you two coming." He looks to Dejan and Remy.

"Sir." Remy salutes and Dejan kind of waves his hand where it's still propped against Remy's shoulder.

"Sit."

Dejan slides into a chair with a faint sigh of relief.

"Corporal, you look like hell."

"Thank you, sir." Dejan offers a formal salute.

"You stay up for us, sir?" Cieran sets down the extra pack and hooks hands in his tac vest collar.

"Your team's been causing some headaches this last year, Sergeant. Wanted to make sure you actually got in."

"Tell me about it," Cieran scoffs lightly. We're not arguing. Our first mission to the Wastelands went off course, then I got targeted by a sorcerer a few months later, then Remy's fae ex from hell showed up, and now Dejan's cousin is out for blood.

The faint twitch to Wolfe's mouth is the closest he usually gets to a real smile, but he sobers as Eckhart knocks on the door and leans in. "He's here, sir."

We all adjust to face the door as it admits a stocky elf in faded jeans, heavy boots, and a scuffed leather jacket with collar turned up against the outside chill.

"Sergeant," Wolfe greets him. The elf salutes and then pivots to clasp Cieran's hand.

"Ylan, what are you doing here?" Cieran asks. Sergeant Ylan Larsen runs a deep cover squad, and if he's here in the CO's office while we are…that's not a good sign.

"You out?"

Ylan shakes his head at Cir's next question. "No, still in deep but got a problem." His soft Texas accent cushions the words. Wolfe doesn't look surprised, and doesn't say anything as Ylan moves further into the room to better face off with us.

He studies Dejan for a moment, dark silver-green eyes crinkling further in his semi-perpetual squint. "That's explaining a lot." He gestures at Dejan.

"But you're not," Dejan beats Cieran to it. Cir and Ylan have known each other for years serving in the same enlisted forces platoon before testing into the Drax Guard. And Ylan is one of the few that Dejan will count as friends outside our squad. And it's mostly because the stocky elf is quiet and very much a ride-or-die type of guy.

Ylan tips a glance at Wolfe and then sits against the corner of his desk. Reckless too, the way he's using the captain's desk as a seat. But Wolfe doesn't say anything, which might be more surprising. This must be really bad news.

"We're in with Klein's crew," he starts.

Cieran shifts between his feet. "Shit, Ylan." He must know more than we do, but even people safe and cozy in residential houses know Klein's name. He's the West Coast version of the Shrikes.

A humorless smile touches Ylan's face. "We've been in for months, and we're finally getting somewhere." His arms cross tight over his chest. "But forty-eight hours ago, Da'mirchen Kostic of the Shrike clan walked into Klein's office."

He pins Dejan with a look and the elf drops a few expletives in elvish that have Ylan giving the same grim smile.

"I'd wondered if there was a connection," Ylan says. But he never asked, never pried. He had to have known based on how long he's been in deep cover. He's probably crossed paths with some sort of low-level Shrike goons before.

"Not that many Kostics in the States," Dejan returns.

Ylan's shoulder lifts. "Could be."

Dejan inclines his head slightly. Remy and I exchange a quick glance. We've known Dejan for five years, been through a lot together, and feel like we know him pretty well. But the last few days have kept surprising us in small ways. This is surprising and not, because these are the sort of people Dejan makes friends with. And if he trusts Ylan, then we can keep trusting the elf too.

"Looks like it wasn't a good family reunion." Ylan tips his chin at Dejan.

"You know cousins. Like to beat the crap out of each other," Dejan replies. "What did he want?"

"Oh, the usual. Any and all information on the Guard, equipment, and muscle." Ylan doesn't shift from the desk, even as Wolfe comes around the opposite corner.

"He planning a war?" Cieran asks it lightly.

"I don't think he's stupid enough to go up against the full Allied States Army, but he's out for blood."

"It's even deeper than that," Wolfe cuts in.

Ylan tips his head, and slight motion rocks through him. The first sign of worry. "He's offering insider information on deep cover operatives as his bargaining tool for Klein's support while he's here."

Even I whisper a low curse.

"What's he know?" Cieran asks.

"I'm not sure," Ylan replies. "He's got a flash drive he says holds names. I don't know if we're all on it, I don't know if it's BMA or FBI. All I know is if he hands that over to Klein like he says he will after he gets Dejan, and as many of you three as he can, a lot of people might be *firred*."

"He give any proof that's what it is?" Cieran asks.

Ylan smiles thinly. "Yeah."

Bitter realization hits me. "You said 'if we're *all* on it.'"

The elf glances at me, something haunted catching his eyes for moment. "Yeah. He handed over two names as a show of good faith. Mine, and a woman's."

Cieran lurches forward a step. "You're okay?" Panic lights up his face and a hand goes to his broadsword like he can fight something.

"Yeah." Ylan's reassurance doesn't do much to quiet the simmering unease in the room. "For now, anyway. He's got real names and confirmation that they're embedded in his organization, but nothing else. I was in the office the entire time and came out alive, so they don't know it's me. Klein's not interested in being one-on-one with the Butcher anytime soon, so chances of me being able to keep an eye on them is high. We've got a tap in the office, and the Eyrie's keeping an even closer watch on things."

"Wait," Dejan breaks in. "He knows I'm alive?"

The quiet deepens. From Tara's and Dejan's reports, he'd been fully comatose from the stoneheart when Damir escaped. Dej had thought maybe the Shrikes would be after us in some sort of revenge if they thought he was dead, but sounds like he's still top of their list.

Ylan nods. "He seemed to think you were alive and well." There's some question in his voice. He must not know everything that went down five days ago.

"Probably the same way those names are on a drive," Cieran says. "There's a leak in multiple places."

The Drax Guard, the FBI, and the Bureau of Magical Affairs don't often share information, and certainly not on their deep cover operatives.

"Damir insinuated he's got someone in the FBI, but I don't know yet how much of that is a bluff or something to try to hold over Klein," Ylan says.

Wolfe gives a tight nod of agreement. "I'm already running an investigation on our end. Ylan's got it covered with Klein and will send updates if he can. Damir and Klein reached an agreement, so Kostic has his men and equipment for whatever he's planning," he says. "You four will focus on joint task force with the FBI agents coming in tomorrow. Once Kostic finds out that you're back in Dunhare, it's going to start getting messy."

"What's the plan, sir?" Cieran asks. Already trying to shuffle pieces into place to make sure he takes care of the team.

"I'm assuming the FBI will want Kostic captured and as much information as they can get on Klein and the Shrikes."

Dejan scoffs. "They'll be damn lucky to get him alive."

"Sounds like you did a pretty thorough job fifteen years ago. Maybe they're hoping for a repeat," Ylan says.

Dejan shakes his head. "I haven't been sending letters back home since then. I know nothing about the current Shrikes other than when Kostics go head-to-head, it ends with bodies."

It's the same chilling warning he's given since he woke up in the field hospital bed and repeated after Maya's call. We've been up against a lot of bad, but Damir sounds like he might take the prize in ruthlessness.

"You four will stay on base until we get a more accurate read on the threat. We don't know what Kostic knows yet, and until we do, this is the safest place for you. And your families."

Remy's hardest hit by that order, but he doesn't flinch.

"FBI agents will be in first thing tomorrow. So get some sleep and report at eight hundred hours."

Another round of salutes and then he dismisses us. Dejan takes Remy's help up. Once in the hall, Ylan stops Cieran.

"How you doing?" the elf asks.

The three of us move farther down the hall, giving them some privacy. Cieran's posture slumps. It's coming up on the year anniversary of his sister's death. The three of us talked a few days ago about making sure he wasn't alone when it hit. How to offer support other than just showing up at the house. Even after a year, we're still trying to figure out the sergeant who can be a little cagey about stuff.

"Been better. You?" Cieran's reply is still audible.

"Been better," Ylan repeats.

Cir gives a faint smile. "You take care of yourself and your team. We'll handle the rest," he says.

Ylan sticks hands in his jacket pockets. "Beer better be cold next time I come around."

"It will be."

"Might not make it on the day." Tightness mars Ylan's words, and the sudden stiffness in his shoulders marks some deeper history with Cieran's sister.

"It's okay." Some of the same hits Cieran. He taps Ylan's shoulder with a fist. "Take care of yourself."

Ylan returns the gesture. "You, too." Then he moves, passing us with a nod, and then vanishes into the stairwell with barely a creak of the door.

Cieran joins us.

"Slumber party at my place?" Dejan asks wryly. He lives on the base in a small apartment. And we're all suddenly realizing he chose it, not for convenience, but for some added security should his past ever come knocking.

"You okay with that?" Cieran asks. We've never really been to Dejan's place, instead usually at Remy's or Cieran's. Sometimes mine, but I'm in a garage apartment attached to my family's house. It's usually only over there when there's food involved. Our other option for tonight is a barracks room in the tower, and we'd all rather cram into an apartment instead.

"I just need to lie down." A tight smile barely stirs Dejan's features.

Cieran has his pack, I've got his weapons, and Remy's got the elf who's not even protesting as he leans on the warlock as we make our way to his home.

6

BESIM

BY EIGHT HUNDRED HOURS, we're on the third floor of the Drax Guard tower HQ, showered, in clean-ish fatigues, and ready to report. Cieran looks like he didn't sleep, but I'd caught the glimpse of him on his phone in the late-night hours when I rolled over. Probably texting Athina and arguing over whatever's making him drag his feet all of a sudden.

Dejan is definitely better after falling asleep as soon as we got inside his apartment, then a stop at the on-base urgent care to see the doctor on the way over this morning.

Wolfe meets us in the hallway, pointing to a briefing room. "Agents will be here shortly," he says. "They've already been breathing down my neck for any and all details, Corporal." He waves Dejan to a seat and the elf complies, managing not to wince as he lowers gingerly into the seat.

"They didn't get the reports? I know Sarge writes in crayon, but..." Dejan smirks and Cieran lightly knocks the chair as he passes.

"It's two different agents than in your file," Wolfe says, and we all wait out the explanation for that one.

"My records and files have been sealed since signing on," Dejan says. "The original agents' names are in the file so whoever the unlucky CO is could call and report me if I get up to anything shady."

"You haven't pissed off anyone enough in the last eight years?" Remy asks, taking a seat as Wolfe does.

"I've tried," Dejan allows.

"We know anything else, sir?" Cieran asks. He's shifting into more serious sergeant mode, and we mirror.

"The FBI's been on Damir for awhile, but haven't gotten anything to legally stick so he's still free and clear. But they might be looking to bring him in old-fashioned handcuffs and hope something sticks."

Dejan frowns. "Damir's not stupid."

"He left Detroit to come get you," Wolfe says. "From reports, he hasn't openly left the city in at least four years."

"You should be flattered," a new voice cuts in. Eckhart holds the door open and gives us a "good luck" look before ducking out and making way for two FBI agents in black suits and ties.

The lead agent is fae, bits of white dusting his temples, eyes a vibrant grey. Remy sizes him up, more accurately getting a reading on this guy's power than the rest of us without magic. His partner is younger, human, hands stuck in tailored pants pockets, satchel over his shoulder.

"Flattered is definitely what I feel," Dejan says. Like us, he sits more guarded, closing off around the agents. They both scan around the room, taking in all four of us plus Wolfe. The fae has a look that says he's not impressed.

There's not enough chairs at the table for everyone, but we're not offering to grab more. I haven't sat yet, so that's my contribution to the proceedings—leaning against the wall in Cieran's periphery.

"Agent Napier," the fae introduces himself. "This is Agent Cason."

"Mitch." The younger flashes a smile like we're all going to be best friends in the next two minutes. He might have walked into the wrong briefing room.

Napier scowls. "Do they all need to be here?"

A look sweeps between us all, echoed back in Wolfe's even stare. "They're your witnesses, Agent."

"Unless one of them is Doctor Tara Novak, I don't think so."

"She's going to be devastated to miss out on meeting you." Dejan presses his mouth in a tight line, not apologetic at all when Wolfe shoots him a look. Our CO introduces us, and Cason intervenes with the satchel before more lines can be drawn.

It *thunks* down on the table, and he pulls out a tablet and several file folders, a thick one last. "This is the file from fifteen years ago." He taps the weighty file. "And this is everything in the intervening years." The other three folders are painfully thin compared to the first folder.

"Where are the original agents?" Dejan asks, his Detroit accent flaring for a second. It's bothering him that it's someone new.

"Dead, or retired a few months ago," is Napier's crisp answer.

"And no one thought to update me?" Wolfe asked.

"You can update his file now. It'll be us."

Dejan crosses his arms, refusal sparking in his tense jaw like he's got any say in this. Between Cieran's and Wolfe's looks, he's going to have to put up with it.

"Let's review this contact Kostic and his lieutenant made yesterday." Napier cuts right to business. Unfortunately, that's me. I don't want to pull Maya, and potentially my sister by association, further into this.

I restate the report I sent to Wolfe yesterday. Napier steeples his fingers together, eyes narrowing. "And you think this Maya Lyons is trustworthy?" he asks.

My hackles rise at the open suspicion, but it's only asking the same nagging question in the back of my mind since I answered the phone.

"She seemed genuine," I say.

"And your relationship with her?"

None of the guys look at me. It's not the time for teasing, not when we've got the FBI agents squaring up for battle.

"Friends."

Napier hums, hands not dropping from their positioning as he leans forward to rest elbows on the table. Fae have an unfortunate ability to sense out lies and truth—a side effect of their direct access to wild magic coating the natural world and pooling in reservoirs. Back in the early Middle Centuries they used to be strictly bound to truth-telling before the Courts were shattered. The event halved their power and actually gave them a lifespan of around four hundred years instead of essentially immortality.

"You don't think she'd try to manipulate you?"

My arms slide across my chest, the action almost unconscious. Another thought that's crossed my mind. I hate it. I hate to even think it, because it's *Maya*. But really, how well do we know each other?

"No." It slips out, like my heart is trying to get a word in edgewise before my brain can take the lead. Napier just hums again and looks to the team.

Cieran shrugs. "If Bes trusts her, then she's solid."

"Cute," Napier almost spits, and Dejan's shoulders twitch. Remy's look bores into the side of our teammate's head until Dejan senses it and glances the warlock's way. The only acknowledgment is a slight narrowing of Dejan's eyes.

It's good to see them back in step. All three of us are still kicking ourselves for not admitting how bad Dejan had gotten with the stoneheart, but now that he's back it's like I didn't realize how *expressive* he is.

For a medic, Dejan can be very stabby. Remy buffers for him most of the time, and I'm the mediator between them and everyone else. Because sometimes the two of them will have competitions for the quietest soldier around.

"Either way, she's staying as far away from this as possible." Cieran steps in. Even if I hadn't admitted to...whatever it is between Maya and me, she's a civilian and Damir Kostic's brutality has already been adequately displayed for us.

"She might be a tool for us—"

"You *firren* kidding me?" Dejan cuts off the fae, and it's a halfhearted "Corporal" from Wolfe in response. Dejan leans forward, seething without any trace of pain. "She came out here to get away from the Shrikes. We're not playing Damir's game and getting a civilian caught in the cross-casting."

Napier smiles thinly. "Good."

The switch as he sits back in his chair is so abrupt that we all stare. Cason offers that same apologetic smile like he knew it was bad cop the entire time. Maybe he did.

Napier stands in sharp motion, the chair rolling away in protest as he starts to pace on his end of the room.

"I'll cut straight with you and your team, Captain. I am not here to make friends." His hand lifts in a dismissive wave of the look we shoot among ourselves again. "I'm here to make sure that Da'mirchen Kostic is behind bars as cleanly as possible."

"We can agree on that," Dejan says. "You could have cut the *ancrit* theatrics."

"The Drax Guard reputation precedes them, much like the FBI," Napier allows. "But consider what I have. A civilian making contact with the very team who crossed paths with Kostic in the Wastelands not five days before. I have the Butcher's cousin sitting in front of me as part of that same team. Where do alliances fall?"

"If you'd read my file, you'd *firren* know," Dejan growls. He subsides with Cieran's quick tap to his forearm. I don't know that our old sergeant Pothos Allaire could have gotten him to stand down so fast. But it's been a heck of a year with Cieran in the lead.

"Things change, and from the reports, you had a hell of a reunion with him," Cason butts in.

Dejan's narrow glare turns to him. "No amount of hugging it out is going to fix whatever relationship Damir and I don't have. This doesn't end until I'm six feet under. Or he is."

The sobering words lay out in the open for five seconds before Cason unlocks his tablet and pulls something from his satchel. "We haven't gotten any eyes on since we got the alert that he's in the city. But it's only a matter of time."

"There's no known Shrike presence in Dunhare." Napier resumes pacing. "And our field agents in Detroit haven't reported any changes. It's very likely that Damir will be recruiting from local gangs."

"Harder to tie anything back to himself," Cieran says, and the agent tips his head.

"He did it in Dallas five years ago and left a muddy trail behind him. It's very likely he'll follow the same pattern." Napier halts long enough to push the chair back to the table, stacking his hands atop it. "We have some field agents embedded in some of the local gangs. We think Klein is the best bet for men."

"We have an active deep cover team in the city. They've confirmed contact has been made with Klein." Wolfe won't give specifics, just like they won't tell us where their agents are.

"Where are your agents?" Cason asks, and gets the full force of ex-pressionless *you messed up* Captain Wolfe. The agent spreads his hands. "Coordination will be key here, and we'll need all the information we can get."

"I'll pass any pertinent information to you," Wolfe says. "And I expect reciprocation."

Napier nods. "You'll get it, Captain."

But Cason turns back to his tablet, mouth flattening slightly as he picks up what I can now identify as a burner phone. He connects it to the tablet with a cord, and I take a step forward. This burner is for someone involved in this case and I'm not letting someone else run all the tech.

Cason glances up at me, and tries to angle the tablet away. I don't usually use my height or bulk to threaten or intimidate, and the fact that I'm using it against this seated agent after about ten minutes is not a good sign for anyone.

"Communications Specialist," I say flatly.

He huffs. "A way for Maya Lyons to contact us. It's safest to assume her phone is tapped. And they'll be expecting some update from her, correct?"

He's uploading a tracker onto the phone. It's a GPS that can easily be disabled if you know what you're doing. I don't answer his question, so Cieran affirms. I don't want to pull Maya into this.

"It will be easiest to have her initiate contact, and then odds are good that she'll be left out of it."

"I don't like the chance." Cieran voices my complaint. Dejan shakes his head. Tara was going to be used against him or against her family and he's not letting anyone else get pulled into this. My feelings don't even matter.

"I've put a contact in here if she needs to get ahold of us." Cason hands it to me. "One of you can get it to her, have her make contact with Kostic, and we'll monitor from there."

"That's a terrible plan," Dejan snaps, restless in his chair.

"You're not moving anywhere fast, Corporal," Napier says. "We'll start the game on his terms while you lie low. She might be able to get us some more intel."

"She's not trained for anything like that," I say, tension rock-hard in my shoulders. My skin tingles, stoneskin trying to push through to protect me and the more easily damaged human skin from threats.

"I've confirmed a protective detail on her, Specialist." Wolfe claims my attention. "Your crew is working with the agents to make sure the Shrikes' focus stays on you four. Objective includes keeping civilians safe and trying to keep this war to a minimum."

I don't like it, but I have no choice. I'm outranked and outvoted. All I can do is try to make sure Maya stays safe. And that starts with checking anything and everything on this phone.

7

MAYA

"What's going on?" my boss, and best friend's, voice jerks me from where I've been polishing the same section of counter for way too long. Nadire Antilles watches me, arms crossed over her *Fox and Ground* apron, her expression similar to the quiet one her brother gives when he senses something is up.

I jerk my thoughts from Besim like that can summon him and Damir Kostic. "Nothing."

Nadi arches her brow and doesn't relent. But I'm not dragging her into this. The safest she's going to be is far away from me, and honestly? I hate having called Besim. That was forty-eight hours ago, and I've heard nothing. From Emmett or from Besim. I don't really know what I was expecting. Crew Six is on mission, and he said he'd call when he could, but...

"Okay, fine. Tests and papers are coming up fast," I say. It's technically true. The end of the fall semester is finally in sight, which means work is increasing and professors are looking for perfection. I'm in my second year toward an architecture degree and now we're combining how to design with magic and without.

"Do you need shift swaps or anything?" she asks. She'll never admit this to anyone, but she's finally getting the shop off the ground. Making the news for being the epicenter of a terrorist attack and people knowing she's related to one of the Drax Guard has brought in a lot more business.

She's also finally charging what she needs to for drinks and the amazing pastries her sister Elsie brings in. Even if she lets first responders and military get free or significantly discounted drinks. It's either the best business plan or she has incredibly high confidence in a mediocre plan, and I haven't decided which. Either way, Nadire doesn't give up.

Which leads me back to trying to throw her off the scent. "No, I should be good. And no sneakily paying for extra hours or 'overtime.'" I point at her.

She spreads her hands with an innocent smile. It lights up her tanned features, and makes her six-foot-one build less intimidating. My half-fae blood gives me a little extra height, but I'm still about four inches shorter, and really feel like a shorty-pants around her family. Trolls, and therefore half-trolls, are all over six foot, built, can be incredibly intimidating, but dang, if her whole family isn't the same generous, welcoming, *kind* sort of people that I want to be when I grow up.

"Just let me know what you need."

I give a thumbs-up and try not to wince. I'm supposed to be acting normal. And I definitely can't tell her that I need my brother and his insane boss to leave. Or more accurately, go to jail where they can't destroy anything else.

Nadi moves off to help a new customer, chatting amiably as she takes the order. That's usually my job—be the friendly one, get to know people a little. Feel a little more free in this life I'm building. But now I'm fading back to the Detroit version of myself that just sort of kept her head down and avoided anyone I knew who had ties to the Shrikes. Which, in my old neighborhood, was almost everyone.

I pull my phone out of my back pocket to check. No new messages, no calls, nothing. I don't know what I'm expecting—Emmett demanding updates, or Besim texting. It's so stupid, but I like that he starts off every conversation with "Hey," and a question that's either about my day or something random that never fails to make me laugh.

Fates, this is either "really good friends," or "everyone brace, they're totally oblivious," and I've read and watched enough rom-coms that I should know. A softly frustrated grumble breaks from me, and I resist the urge to smack the phone against my forehead.

"Who's texting you?"

I yelp, and automatically angle away from Nadi. For a half-troll she is a freaking ninja.

"Or not texting you?" She wiggles her eyebrows, and I narrow my eyes back.

Part of the reason her brother is *Commander Ryder* in my phone is to avoid the interference of one Nadire Antilles.

"Come on, let me live vicariously through you," she complains good-naturedly.

I allow a smile. It's what I told her months ago when she was pining after Remy Kalama. But she's over him now, and we're both part of the betting pool on when he's going to ask out that Bureau agent. They've been here at the same time before and it was almost painfully cute to watch them.

"There's no one," I say. Technically true.

Nadi glances around, lowers her voice conspiratorially, and says, "Do you want me to make Besim ask you out?"

Heat sears my face, and I almost jump away. "Oh my—No! *What*?"

She practically cackles in response. I'm still trying to...I don't know, deny something. But she cuts me off with hands to my shoulders.

"Maya, I'm an expert on pining, and my brother cannot take his eyes off you when he comes in. And you are like ten times happier when he does. So..." Her eyebrows wiggle again, and I sigh, melodramatically.

"I don't know what you mean."

Her smirk tells me she sees right through it, much like she probably has since day one of us texting. The bell dings and she glances to the door, her face lighting up.

"Let's ask him right now."

My head turns so fast that loose curls try to obscure my vision. And I wish they had. Because Besim just walked in, smiling like nothing has happened and he hasn't been gone for weeks. Nadi hurries around the counter, grabbing him in a hug, before trying to push him toward me. But I'm rooted to the ground, anchored by the dread tumbling in my gut.

He wasn't supposed to come *here*. He was supposed to text. He wasn't supposed to look me in the eye and let me betray him and his team.

Besim steps around the counter, coming face-to-face with me, and I can only stare up at him. Tension writhes in my chest and tries to escape in bursts of vibrant grey magic to shove him out the door and far, far away from me.

"Hey," he says softly, and I want to burst into tears. So I dodge around him and make for the back entrance. If I can't see him, and I block his number, then I can't pass anything on to Emmett.

Nadi's surprise follows me, but I ignore it. I'm three steps down the alley, apparently just about to race away from my shift and the four hours I've got left, when Besim's deep voice calls after me, and my traitor feet stop. Turn around. And don't move when his military boots come toe-to-toe with my Kelly-green sneakers.

"Maya?"

"Why did you come *here*?" I manage through tight throat and clenched jaw.

"To make sure you were okay."

Our shoes swim through suddenly watering eyes. His hand gently touches my forearm, and my shoulders slack downward. I sniff and manage to look up at him. He's in dark grey fatigues, Allied States flag patch on his right sleeve and coiled red fire drake grabbing a sword on his left. The words *Fear No Fire* should be inspiring, but they kind of make me mad and scared that he just might jump into fire again for me.

"What do you think?" I try to hold him off with a slightly harsher tone. But he just arches an eyebrow, calling my BS.

He glances at some point over my shoulder. "Rem," he says almost conversationally. The ripple of someone else's magic swoops over us. I tense until I recognize the barrier of a silence well. We'll be blocked from any external eavesdropping, like the coffee shop owner standing in the back door watching us.

"We're not just letting you face off with them alone, okay?" he says, and new tears form in my eyes. "Can I see your phone? Please?"

"Are we doing a jealous boyfriend routine?" I muster the words, already fishing it out.

The eyebrow arches and a faint smile quirks. Teasing. "Ask me out first before calling me a boyfriend."

It gets a chuckle, and I scrub my nose as he skims through my phone. Although I can't help but notice it seems like the sort of thing uninterested friends would say as a joke.

"What are you looking for?" I ask.

"Seeing if they tapped your phone at all."

I freeze. Should I have thought of that? What if I *really* messed up by calling him?

"Don't beat yourself up about calling. I'm really glad you did," he says like he can sense the thoughts burning rubber through my head.

"Are you?" I cross my arms tight across my chest.

"Yeah. Otherwise we'd have walked in blind." He's serious and a little guilt falls from me. "This your brother?" He tips the phone to me, showing the new contact pinned to the top of my messages. I nod, and he pulls out his phone and copies over the number.

"What are you doing?" I ask as he keeps typing something in my phone.

"Nerd stuff." He tips another smile, but it's not quite reaching his eyes. He hands my phone back, then pulls a burner phone out of the front pocket of his shirt. "Keep that somewhere safe. It's got all our contacts in it, and got enough dampeners on it that magic shouldn't shut it down."

I stick it into my apron pocket. That's not the definition of "safe" but it's less conspicuous than a pocket and it'll do for now.

"Someone's going to be around keeping an eye on you and the shop."

I take a shaky breath. "Who?"

"The less you know, the better." He offers an apologetic tilt of the head. I wave it off. That's fair. "But anyone who uses the code word *Artemis* can be trusted."

He smirks a little as I arch my brow at him. That's the rebel safe house we were trying to make it to during our *Starfall* game night. The one we didn't make it to because he blew our cover. We didn't have time to finish because real life got in the way.

"Text your brother and let him know that we're back in town."

"Bes, I can't—"

His hand against my arm cuts me off. "You can. Look, after this, we're hoping that they leave you alone. I just need you to stay safe, okay?"

There's a look in his eyes that makes me afraid and reckless all at once. "You too," I say.

He smiles and my heart kickflips. Before I can say or do anything stupid, like hug him, he steps around me and the spell hiding our words falls.

"Contact us if anything happens," he says and then he's gone, striding down the alley and vanishing around the corner.

"What. The. Hell?" Nadi is at my side in a moment, her face somewhere between confused and pissed. I'm not sure if that's directed at me or her brother.

I smile weakly, and then really do start crying.

8

MAYA

Nadire practically drags me back inside the café, waving off the college-age employee watching in concern. We go into the small office, and she points to the hideous yellow swiveling chair that's way too comfy to be that color. I sink into it and take a tissue from the extended box.

She displays sudden patience as I blow my nose twice, and then a third time in an attempt to stall. It doesn't work. Nadi's arms cross, and I focus on the crumpled tissues balled between my hands.

"My brother showed up the other day," I finally say.

"The no-good one?"

"I only have one." The tissues receive my miserable smile. "And he's into really bad stuff."

"And what's that got to do with Besim?"

I raise my head and give her a *wait* look that she's used to getting from me. She returns it with the *talk faster* look I usually get from her.

"Whatever he's here for, it involves the crew somehow." I hedge around the real answer. "He wanted me to tell him when I see Besim or any of the crew again. They know he's your brother and that he comes around."

Unease creases Nadi's face and she moves only to nudge the trashcan around the desk with her foot, bringing it into range for me to offload the tissues.

"And I called Bes after my brother left, and..."

"And the idiot came here to let everyone know they're back in town and jump right into whatever new dangerous thing?" Nadi finishes.

I nod miserably and take another tissue to blow my nose with a truly disgusting noise. Nadi doesn't flinch other than to move some of the precarious stacks of paper in her "file system" so she can sit on the edge of the desk.

"I'm really sorry I dragged him into trouble, and I'm really sorry if something happens here again and—"

She holds up her hand, cutting me off. "Hey, I accidentally pulled you into 'terrorists in the coffee shop' months ago. I'm not judging. And I also know to trust my brother and his team." Her shoulders slump. "I'm going to be praying *so* many rosaries," she mutters.

I smile weakly. The Antilleses are all faithfully Catholic, and the best kind who actually live out their faith alongside their actions. It's one more thing to like about Besim, even if I'm not sure on the whole religion thing. My parents really weren't, and then when you've got a brother in one of the worst criminal organizations in the country and hear about some awful things happening...it's hard to believe in Eternal Goodness.

But if anyone can convince me to try, it might be Besim and his entire family.

"Say one or two for me?" I ask. I kind of know the concept behind the prayer, but I definitely know if you put Marie Antilles in charge of any prayer, she'll be storming heaven until she gets an answer. But I don't want her to know anything about this because I really don't want to lose her genuine warmth and hospitality after I dragged her son into danger. Again.

"Maya, you are the primary recipient of these," Nadi says.

"Don't tell your mom."

Nadire huffs. "Oh, my lips are already sealed, and you know that takes some doing."

A faint chuckle makes it through, and I snag another tissue.

"Did he have any plan or say anything?" she asks quietly.

"Just to let them know if my brother or anyone else shows up. They're hoping that I'll be out of the way once..." Once I make a phone call to Emmett. But what if I never do?

"This is sounding depressingly familiar."

We share a grim smile. It's about exactly what they told us to do after a sorcerer walked into the *Fox*. And that didn't turn out very well. Or about as well as it could have, depending on how you look at it.

I should tell her that someone is supposed to be around keeping an eye on me. But I'm already going to be suspicious of anyone coming in who's not a regular, and I don't need Nadi also asking each customer painfully leading questions to see if we can ferret anyone out.

"You sure you don't need anything?" Nadi leans a little closer, but even with her on the desk and me in the troll-sized chair, it doesn't feel like she's looming over me.

"Just for everything to be done and Besim to be safe." Stinging hits my nose again. If anything happens, I might not forgive myself.

"So..." she starts with a glint in her eyes that I don't like. "You and Besim...?"

"Nope." I stand and toss the tissues. She laughs as I shake my head. "I'm not answering any further questions at this time."

"Maya." She snags my apron edge long enough to halt me. "Seriously, we'd all be more than happy if anything happened with you two, so don't feel weird or anything..."

I shove hands in my apron pocket, fingers closing around the burner phone. My shoulders slump at the contact. "And what if *my* family drags him and the team into something horrible? It's...my brother runs with some really bad people, Nadi. I..."

"Hey." She slides off the table and drapes an arm around my shoulders. I lean into the side-hug.

"You got any more prayers?" I sniff.

She huffs. "We're Catholic. Of course we do."

A faint laugh edges its way out, and I withdraw from the hug only to grab more tissues. "I might need a few minutes before going back out. Don't want to scare customers away."

"If you need to leave, you can. Although, is that safe?"

"I don't really know anymore." Tears make a frantic attempt to escape, and I inhale shakily, barely keeping them at bay. "But I have some defensive spells to use in a pinch," I reassure. I grew up around Detroit's gang side and have walked through some pretty shady areas in my time.

"That makes me feel slightly better," she says. "But I might be enforcing a buddy system. You are going to be sick of me."

I chuckle. It's been awhile since I've had a really good friend. Just having someone around is lessening some of the crushing terror.

"Never." I dab my eyes. "I promise to text you when I get home, et cetera."

"You better." She levels a finger at me. "Are you taking the afternoon off, or do you want to hang around here?"

I shrug. "I don't know. No option sounds very good."

"How about I make you some hot chocolate and then you decide?"

Fox and Ground hot cocoa is always a good idea. She heads out, and I take another few seconds to blow my nose and wash my hands before joining her. The other employee, a half-elf with bright purple highlights in her blonde hair, arches a pierced eyebrow.

I wave my hand in reassurance. "Family drama."

She nods. "My sympathies. I have boyfriend drama. Wanna switch?"

"No thanks." I chuckle. "But let me know what advice you want. I can tell you to dump him or give him another chance."

The half-elf quirks a grin. "I've already decided to break up, just have to figure out how to do it."

"Oof." I pat her shoulder. "Good luck."

"Thanks. And you know, you don't have to stick with family just because they're blood." A bit of chagrin fills her face and she points to her ears. Right. Like fae, elven hearing is twice that of humans, and half-elves usually get it too.

"Yeah." I scuff my sneaker against the tile floor. "But it's hard to figure out how to tell someone that."

"Good luck." She offers a smile and makes way for Nadi and a mug of hot cocoa.

"Go sit." Nadi hands it off. She's finally been able to get grey stoneware mugs with the café logo—a Nordic knotwork fox leaping over a steaming coffee mug—etched in white relief, and they've been a pretty big hit with the regulars.

I take the hot cocoa, topped with whipped cream and dusted with cinnamon, over to the high-top table and slide up onto the chair. It's one of the tables sized for taller humans or trolls, but it's nearest the service counter and has the best view of the shop. And the best space to spread out study material during slower periods.

Guess I'm off the clock for however long it takes me to finish this and decide if I'm going home or not. Or if I'm calling Emmett or not. But the memory of Damir Kostic's flat eyes sends a chill right through me. Refusing contact is probably how I end up gutted in an alley.

My hands curl around the mug like that's going to save me. The bell dings and a guy in a layered hoodie and leather jacket comes partially in.

"Dogs okay inside?" he asks.

"Sure!" Nadi replies. She's already leaning forward to get first look at the dog he's going to bring in. He flashes a smile and shoves the door open wider and a Celtican wolfhound pads in at his side.

Full fae are basically just wild magic transmitters and can feel the presence of it all around, and therefore can sense other magic users. They're the most powerful magic users, able to refine sometimes volatile wild magic in their bodies before casting. Half-fae like me always have magic. So I can tell that this guy is a warlock. They always have a different feel to their magic, something pulsing around them like magic is smug to live in their veins and not just flow through like it has to with fae.

The warlock pushes back his hood, exposing dark hair and features creased in a perpetual smile. He's a little stocky through the shoulders and moves with that soft grace that I've noticed around Besim and the team. The wolfhound stops beside him at the counter. A very loose slip-leash circles its neck. That dog is big enough to see over the counter on all four paws, so it better be as well-behaved as the leash suggests.

Nadi's asking about it, and the guy answers in a broad New Jersey accent, maybe flirting a little as he does. Nadi's not batting an eye. It looks around, nose twitching. It focuses on me, intelligent eyes meeting mine. Something about it makes my magic tingle. But since no one else is attacking this guy for putting a shifter in animal form on a leash, maybe I'm just getting a misread with the nearby warlock magic.

"What's his name?" Nadi props hands on the counter, leaning over like she really needs more height to see over the edge at the giant dog.

"Charming."

The wolfhound breaks off its stare and looks up at the warlock like he's personally affronted by the name. I'd be too.

The guy laughs with Nadi, spreading his hands. "Don't look at me. He came with the name."

"What can I get you and Charming?" she asks.

He orders the toffeenut latte and I smile like I do every time. It's a popular one at the shop, and one that I experimented with last winter after working here for a few weeks. My smile dies just as fast. I should put distance between myself and the shop, Nadi, and everyone else.

"Nothing for Charming, but I'm on the way to meet a friend, and he'll have a vanilla latte."

Charming growls and the warlock nudges him with a knee. They head closer to me to wait for drinks and the wolfhound edges closer.

"Hey," the guy chides but doesn't pull.

"It's okay." I lean forward in the chair. Since fae are basically just extensions of nature and magic, animals are usually pretty comfortable around fae and half-fae. I hold out a hand and the wolfhound sniffs, then withdraws.

Even closer, I'm still not sure if he's a shifter or not, so I'm not going to risk it and ask to pet him. Most shifters usually don't wander around public places in their animal form, and it's been a lifelong phobia of mine to accidentally offend one by trying to pet them.

Although most shifters are some sort of non-domestic animal, like wolves or bears, or dragons like Sergeant O'Donnell's girlfriend. But still.

"I should have gotten whatever that is." He nods at my mug, the whipped cream starting to melt into the chocolate. I've barely taken two sips and it's still steaming.

"Hot cocoa," I say. "You'll have to come back and try it."

He chuckles and I can almost feel something like a summer breeze. Air warlock. Usually I like trying to assess other people's magic. Elves are easy. If their features and eyes don't give them away, all have magic based off *regeneration* and *nurture*. Warlocks have so many gradients, it's fun. But now with the threat of Emmett and the Shrikes around, as well as a mysterious "someone" around to keep an eye on me, it's just making me want to pull up defensive wards.

"I don't make it over to this side of town very often, but I might make an exception."

Charming sinks politely down to haunches, nose twitching again. He's got a blotch of white just off-center on his chest, and a furrow through the fur on his right shoulder that must be from some scar tissue.

"He seems nice." I nod at the wolfhound, still unsure enough that I'm not about to call him a *good boy*.

"He's not bad to have around." The warlock grins and the wolfhound cranes a look up at him.

"Does he disagree?" I ask with the hint of a smile.

"More than likely." He grabs the coffee cups and smiles at Nadi. She's used to flirty guys, so she just offers a wave and a "come back and see us."

I hop off the chair, beating him to the door to open it so he doesn't have to juggle both cups and the leash.

"See you around," he says, and a friendly smile and wink leave me convinced that I just might be seeing him and this wolfhound again.

67

9

Besim

"I feel like a jerk." I slide into Remy's old green Explorer parked across the street and down from the café and slam the door shut. He arches an eyebrow and starts the engine. He barely beat me back to the car from the alley.

"For trying to protect someone?" he asks.

I glare out the windshield, and he huffs.

"I have no advice for you, since it's clear I'm terrible with relationships. I either pick the absolute worst, or can't figure out how to ask the best."

I slouch back into the seat. "The first one wasn't your fault," I remind him, and will keep reminding him until the day we die, since it's not likely he's going to forgive himself for it before then.

He doesn't say anything, and I don't either as I grab my tablet and pair it with my phone. I took *Emmett Lyon's* contact info from Maya's phone and activated a GPS tracker on her phone and shared it to mine. Kind of like a stalker, since I didn't tell her.

"She have the burner?" Remy asks.

I nod. The phone that Agent Cason programmed and I checked and double-checked. It's still got his contact info in it, but it also has ours. It was a gamble we decided to take in a meeting after leaving the FBI agents.

If anything happens with that phone, our information might get into the wrong hands.

Dejan's ready to give the agents a double middle finger, but we're all stuck in this since it's going to be a losing battle to find an FBI agent we like to work with.

The tracker will let me keep an eye on it, and her. I'm really hoping that I'll never have to use it, or the alert that will notify me if her brother contacts her.

I should have just told her.

"At least you're not tapped into the phone of the person you'll at least admit to liking," I say.

Remy chuckles. "I think there's a difference between making sure she doesn't get kidnapped by a drug lord and making sure no other guy ever talks to her."

"What if I turn obsessive?"

Remy just gives me a flat look. It kills some of the paranoia, but not quite the underlying fear. "Bes, you've never once been that way, and no one in your family is either."

I'm still trying to figure out the root cause of the hesitation because I hate this.

"Afraid you'll ruin your one chance with someone because of something you did?" he asks wryly.

Some of the tension eases. "Yeah. That."

"Then just tell her." Remy tips an elbow against the car window, watching the street and the hooded guy walking into the coffee shop with a wolfhound in tow. Specialist Tommy Corsetti is always right on time.

"Is that advice for me or for you?" I ask. I've really been around him and Dejan too long since I'm becoming better at deflecting and taking a turn at being the stubborn one.

Remy doesn't turn his attention from the shop, just moves his arm to flash a rude sign that makes me chuckle. But he's right. I just need to tell her. But how to do that when a few minutes ago was the last time we'll be seen around this café, and I won't be texting her in case I'm not the only one who's tampered with her phone? That burner is only for emergencies.

"How's it going?" Cieran's voice breaks in over the comms. He's been in meetings with Wolfe and the agents and must have just stepped away to get an update. Dejan's hopefully sleeping since the base is still determined to be the safest place to lie as low as possible until Damir makes a move. But knowing him, he's probably perched somewhere and doing something he's not supposed to be doing.

"On schedule," I reply. One of Ylan's team agreed to make some time to shadow Maya for a few days just to make sure that she stays out of the crossfire. And he'll be a lot more unobtrusive than anyone else.

"Good," Cieran replies shortly. We have code names and actual names for the entire deep cover team, but nothing over open channels unless needed. The FBI has their list of contingency plans, and we've got our separate ones. A few might even overlap with the agents. This is turning into something too big to keep all the eggs in one basket. Klein and his gang, Kostic and the Shrikes, undercover operatives in both, and Dejan the centerpiece.

"How are meetings?" I ask.

"How do you think?" he retorts. Remy and I both grin. I might feel slightly sorry for the FBI agents having to deal with Cieran before he's had at least two cups of coffee.

"I can join," Dejan cuts in. He's not supposed to even be on comms, but none of us are surprised.

"Tempting," Cieran replies.

"I don't want to fight World War Three," Remy says.

Dejan snorts. "Don't be a baby."

Remy smirks, and I just shake my head.

"I think I might end up missing those glorious three months where Dejan wasn't a complete maniac," I say.

A low laugh is Dejan's answer. "I've got lots of time to catch up on."

"That's what concerns me," Cieran butts in.

Remy's silent. At least until Dejan speaks again. "Bes, punch Remy for me since he's probably staring dramatically into the middle distance."

"And destroy this majestic and brooding profile?" I *tsk*.

The warlock's lips twist against a smile. Up the street, Tommy re-emerges with two coffee cups stacked atop each other, and the wolfhound beside him. Maya waves after them where she's holding the door. Guilt pricks again, but I can't do anything as the door swings closed and folds her back into the café.

Tommy flicks a glance and a slight tilt of his chin in our direction. They disappear around the corner and seconds later, a different man in ratty jeans, thick jacket, and beanie emerges holding a *Fox and Ground* cup. He crosses the street and takes to one of the benches sheltered under spidery leafless trees—one that gives him a good view of the café.

A minute later, Tommy reappears, pulling hood back over his head as he crosses the street. He holds his cup carelessly, other hand stuck in his jacket pocket as he strides past our car without acknowledging and heads up the sidewalk, disappearing at the street corner into the waiting bus.

"I couldn't do what they do." Remy shakes his head. "Even without a kid."

I check the side mirror view of the now on-duty deep cover member. He leans on his knees, cup spinning between his hands.

There's different kinds of quiet when it comes to soldiers. The Guard gets the toughest missions, and we don't talk about it outside of other teams. Sometimes not even then, compartmentalizing to try to keep some things separate from living rooms and city streets and coffee shops. But sometimes, especially right after missions, it's hard not to just sit in unfocused silence.

The deep cover crew has a different sort of silence when they're around. An extra lethal edge to it. They spend months, sometimes years, in the muck of humanity to come out the other side hopefully having done some good after it all.

Ylan's tried to recruit Dejan onto his team before, but Dej has always refused. He could probably do it, but after hearing his story, he's already experienced living something like a double life deep in a gang's infrastructure. He's deadly with weapons, but he clings tightly to his medic side, the part he trained to help people and make something better after years of the opposite.

I couldn't do it either, with the leaving for months or years without contact, identity changed, becoming a different person. It's hard enough to leave my family with unexpected notice for indeterminate amounts of time. But at least there's the promise that I'll always be me the whole time.

Though maybe they can't really do it all either. We crossed paths with Tommy months ago when Janvier was after me. He wasn't doing so good mentally, letting his cover slip for just a second. I'd given him a St. George medal. I figure dragon slayers are good patrons for the Drax Guard. And Tommy's still been on the same case since then.

The bus is long gone, and his partner still sits on the bench. Remy shifts the car into gear and pulls out.

10

MAYA

I LINGER AT THE door for just a moment longer, wishing I could run out and keep running and leave everything behind. Instead, the weight in my stomach grows heavier and heavier, keeping me in place.

"Maya?" Nadi comes to stand beside me. I manage to smile, but my arms wedge tight across my stomach. She touches my shoulder and it's such an open gesture that tears threaten again. I turn with an effort and make my way back to the table where my hot chocolate still sits steaming, whipped cream slowly melting into itself.

Nadire doesn't say anything as she goes back behind the counter. I love hot chocolate. The taste, the sugar, the way the chocolate interacts with my magic and makes me feel energetic. But looking at it, I'm not sure I'll be able to drink it without it tasting like dirt.

I pull my phone out. It spins around and around in my hands, tilting the same arguments over and over. Tell Emmet, don't tell him. There aren't any pros in this situation. Just an increasingly longer list of cons.

Besim and his crew can take care of themselves. He's probably right and once I betray Crew Six, Emmet and Damir won't have much more use for me. I'll be safe. As safe as anyone could be in the orbit of the Shrikes.

But can I do it?

My stomach is layers of knots, twisting and snarling around each other. I never regretted leaving Detroit and settling here. Was starting to dream a little of a future that might include Besim. Even if everyone comes out unscathed from the war that's brewing, there's no way any friendship between us sticks.

Not if I go through with this.

But...it's make the call, or see Nadi suffer. In the end, it might be better to risk the Antilles sibling who has a longsword and a crew that includes two magic users who won't blink twice about fighting criminals, and one sergeant who smiles and laughs until his people are in trouble. And I know Besim would agree with me.

All the same. I can't do it here in Nadi's café. Can't do it in the place where I met Besim and he and his crew protected us before. So I wait until Nadire's busy in the small storeroom to slip out the front door, making sure the door doesn't swing wide enough to disturb the bell and announce my departure. I half run to the corner, dodging around it. My back slams against the wall and it takes two tries to key in my passcode with shaking fingers.

Even longer to type out the simple *-They're back-*.

Tears crowd my eyes and defensive magic swirls in my limbs, trying to fight its way through my hands. It takes a concentrated breath to draw it back. The tears aren't as easy to control, and I mentally tell the Antilleses goodbye as I hit send.

Emmet doesn't even give me time to mourn. *-Good.-*

My heart plummets into the mess of knots that's my stomach at his next text. *-We'll have another job for you. Keep your phone close.-*

I can't answer. Just shove it into my back pocket and head back to the café. Sneak in the back door, and whisper a prayer of thanks to the Fates that Nadi's not in the office as I grab my backpack and keys. One wistful glance around at the café that I'll miss, and then I leave.

———

My tiny studio apartment feels too crowded, too cluttered. I shouldn't have so freely accumulated so much stuff in the last year. I can't possibly take it all with me.

I sit on the back of the armchair and stare at the duffel bag open on the bed, clothes stacked next to it. Leaving Detroit hadn't been this hard. I'd just stuffed clothes and the few things I cared about in the same duffel and headed to the train station. Now it seems like the *Fox and Ground* apron folded at the bed corner, the burner phone tucked underneath it, might be the start of too many important things. Like I can take a coffee shop with me.

Motion tugs my curls, and I take out the small blue butterfly clips. They were Mom's. She was the fae and loved any sort of butterfly. Dad had gotten her these, and she'd enchanted them to move with moods. They always get comments—vibrant blue wings spiderwebbed with dark veins that wiggle when I laugh. It makes me feel closer to her for a few seconds. It's been nine years since they died—sometimes it feels like yesterday and sometimes like a hundred years ago.

One thing I'm thankful for with Dad's human genes is that I won't actually live for four hundred years like full fae. Half-fae live closer to a human life expectancy. A hundred years already seems like too long to live with the heartbreak of losing parents so young, having an estranged brother, and struggling just to make it. I don't want to live with it for four hundred.

I lean forward to set the clips on the bed. My laptop, covered in stickers, sits on the small built-in wall desk. Textbooks and other books

I got from the used bookstore two blocks from the *Fox* lean against each other, or stack in a pile on the edge.

Of course Besim likes some of the same books I do. And even though I can get copies literally anywhere I go, I want to take *these* with me. My arms tuck across my stomach and I lean over them, frustration ripping from me. I need to stop thinking about him. About what might happen to him because I was too scared to say *no*.

A knock brings my heart lurching into my throat. I whip around. It comes again. Insistent. I check my phone. No messages. I'd texted Nadi when I got home, telling her I just left for the day. Unable to tell her I was leaving town for good.

Another knock. Fighting some inane hope that it might be her or Besim, I cross the tiny excuse for a living area and check the peephole. And fall back a step at the sight of Emmet on the other side.

I look around wildly like there's some other exit from the apartment other than a window to a narrow balcony. But before I can commit to anything utterly stupid, the lock clicks and he swings the door open.

I don't have any wards up because I was trying to live as unparanoid as possible. Even if I did, he and I have the same magic, and he'd be able to dismantle them. He's always been better at wards than me.

"You going to invite me in?" he asks, hands in his jeans pockets, like he didn't just use a spell to unlock my door.

"You already invited yourself," I manage, and back further onto the blue rug spotted with bright yellow sunbursts.

He comes in, glances around, jaw set like he might be judging my space. "Going somewhere?" he challenges when his attention makes it back around to me.

I duck around him and shut the door, shooting the deadbolt home.

"Maya." He's patiently aggrieved by my continued silence as I give him a wider berth and brace myself between him and my bag.

"How did you find me?" I finally ask through tight jaw.

Emmet just tilts his head and cocks an eyebrow. I glare back. Guess it was too much to hope that I'd have some sort of privacy in all this.

"Why?" I spit out.

"Why what?" Now he's playing dumb.

I scoff. "You *know* what, Emmet."

Anger flashes in his eyes, spasms across his face. "The Shrikes took care of us, Maya."

I lurch forward a step, matching his anger. "*I* took care of us!" I jam my finger at my chest. "I did, and you didn't care about any of it."

"Where do you think that apartment and the money for it came from, May?"

"I knew where it came from, and I told you to take it all back! I had it figured out." We'd fringed the Shrikes' territory even when Mom and Dad were alive, and they'd warned us not to take anything from them. I'd listened, but apparently it was just a challenge for Emmet. And two years after they died, he'd joined the gang.

"They taught me to use my magic. Mom never did." He tries a different tack.

Another scoff rips free. "It's hard to teach magic when you're dead, Em."

He'd been almost fourteen when they'd died. Everyone learns magic basics in grade school. By high school, magic users have separate classes based on what race or type of caster they are, but it's still just basic casting, wards, charms. Anything bigger or linked to family traditions are taught by parents. High-level or complex casting is taught at university where you can diversify your magic and become a degreed wizard.

I barely got more from Mom than he did. And then I dropped out of school to try to take care of us, and never had the money to pay for classes to get more training. I've had to take some intermediary college classes to get me up to level for some of the architecture classes that integrate magic and design.

My heart takes another hit at that thought. I'll have to withdraw from school. Maybe give up on that dream entirely.

"I'm leaving, Emmet. I'm not letting you use me in any way."

Emmet shakes his head, coming a step closer. A bit of brotherly concern shines in his eyes. "May, you can't..."

"The hell I can't." I retreat a step.

His features tighten again, and for a second, I really do think it's concern. "Maya." An abrupt knock sounds, and he tilts a look over his shoulder. "You can't."

I'm frozen in place as he goes to answer it and admits Damir. I stumble back, knees hitting the edge of the bed and threatening to buckle at the sight of the elf I'd hoped to never see again.

Damir's sharp gaze sweeps around the room, mouth lifting in a slight sneer as he does. I'm found wanting.

"I was starting to think you'd gotten lost, Emmet." His voice is even, patient.

Emmet's eyes narrow at me, like this is all my fault. "Just hashing out old family business, sir."

Damir's thin smile holds no humor. "I know how that is." He prowls a step closer, and I try to physically lean back, but the bed stops me. "Emmet thought you might try to run." He pulls a thin blade from under his sleeve and turns it over in his hands. I swallow hard, mesmerized by the shimmering steel.

"I was hoping you'd be smarter than that." Damir flicks an icy glance my way.

"What...what do you want?" My intention to run seems so unutterably stupid right now. I should have known that I wouldn't have been able to. Face-to-face with Damir, I'm not even sure that Besim and the others could actually protect me.

"I want you to stop lying to me," he says.

My lips clamp shut. I can't even deny it. The Butcher smiles again, and there's a faint glitter in his eyes.

"See? Smart." He sheaths the knife and slides hands into his pockets. I'm not fooled by the casual look. Emmet's crossed his arms over his chest, like he's trying to intimidate. But something about his stance makes me look twice at him. He stands angled, just so slightly, between me and Damir. But I don't know if that means he'd try to protect me in any way.

"I know my cousin is alive." Damir claims my focus again. "Thanks to you, I know they're all back in town. And"—that same cruel smile tugs the corner of his mouth again—"I know that you're in love with Besim Antilles."

My mouth goes dry, blood rushing to pool in my feet.

"Oh," he *tsks*. "Hearts don't lie. And yours sped up any time he came up in conversation a few days ago."

I have no argument. Elvish magic is based on *regeneration* and *nurture*. It's most often tuned for healing. It would be easy for an elf to figure that out, but I guess I hadn't expected Damir Kostic to know anything about healing.

"There are many uses for elvish magic." It's like Damir reads my thoughts. "Many ways it can be used." He glances around, then must decide he doesn't want to sit in the armchair or the barstool that's more of a catch-all for clothes than an extra seat. "What I want to know is what you are to him?"

Just hours ago, I wanted to know. Now I'm glad I don't. "Just a friend."

Damir's head tilts and I feel like crossing arms over my upper chest like that can block out the sound of my heartbeat. If he's not just lying. Fae used to be compulsive truth tellers back when the Courts gave them near limitless power and near immortality. Fae still are more truthful, even centuries after the courts were broken, perhaps something in the access to natural magic creating that check. Half-fae are too. I've always been teased that even my face can't tell a lie. He could have taken a shot in the dark and my stupid self gave the rest away.

"He strikes me as the loyal type." The knife comes out again. "What might he do for a 'friend'? Or a sister?"

"Leave Nadi out of this." I jolt forward a step.

Damir chuckles. "Do they have any idea how loyal of a friend they have in you?" The knife point skims a pattern around my silhouette, and even from five feet away, I can feel the cold brush of steel.

I don't know if they do. All I know is I've been lucky enough to have them as friends.

"I'm here for my cousin," Damir says. "If I can't get him first, then he'll come for one of his team. And it seems like Antilles, or any of them, might use that burdensome sense of duty to protect you. I can't have a piece trying to run off before we might need her. So." He gestures to the door, and I have no choice.

Emmet's look confirms it, and it's a silent plea to just do whatever I'm told. A shudder hits and I obey, walking past the both of them. I look back once at the apartment and—my heart stalls for a second—the burner phone still underneath the apron. My phone is in my back pocket, but who knows if I'll have a chance to use it.

Emmet comes behind me, a handsbreadth away. So he doesn't trust me not to bolt as soon as I can. Smart. He prompts me down the back stairs of the apartment building and out the side door where a dark car is parked.

He opens the back door and silently points in. I balk for another second, arms pinned across my chest.

"May," he whispers, and tilts his head again. I want to ask him how he can stomach doing this? How he feels dragging his only sister into this?

He's always been better at hiding his emotions, been better about obscuring the truth. But right now, I think I have my answer in the regret shining from his grey-ringed eyes.

It might be too late for that. I ignore it and get into the car. A stocky dark-haired elf sits in the driver's seat. He glances my way in the rearview mirror, deep forest green and silver eyes creased in what seems like a perpetual squint. His battered leather jacket collar is flipped up even though the heat is on in the car.

"Buckle, miss," he says, voice husky and tinged with a southern drawl.

Emmet's scoff holds some humor. "You always this cautious, Hunnar?"

I catch Hunnar's faint smile in the rearview again as he watches me then inclines his head to the left. "Can't hurt to be careful."

I use the action of buckling the seatbelt to look out the left windows, immediately feeling stupid. Until I see the grey wolfhound with a blotch of white on his chest lying in the shadow of the apartments across the street. His head is up, front legs braced against the concrete, ready to move. I hastily look away, pretending to adjust the belt over my chest.

Just the hint of something or someone who could help me shakes some of the paralysis from my limbs.

Damir slides in the left door to claim the seat next to me. I inch away until I'm pressed up against the door. He chuckles lightly, seeming much too pleased just for that reaction. He doesn't bother to buckle up, and apparently Hunnar doesn't dare remind *him*.

"Drive," Damir orders, and with a quiet "Yes, sir," Hunnar shifts gears and drives away.

11

Dejan

Someone's in my apartment. I shake off the last dregs of sleep, still with blankets pulled up over my head. It's a bad habit, one that I've carried over from childhood to avoid arguments, loud music, or worse, but one that I still do when I feel safe in my environment.

It takes another second before I smile slightly. Still safe, since I doubt my cousin would have broken in and made Remy's chicken and noodle soup—spicy like all of us prefer—and be joking around with Besim before murdering me in my own bed.

I pull the blankets down and check the clock. Fifteen hundred. I fell asleep shortly after Bes and Remy made the phone drop at the café, and slept for at least two hours. I'm still tired enough to pass out again later tonight.

Everything hurts less as I sit up, and it's been awhile since my last dose of meds and pass with my healing magic. Elves, like shifters and any other magic user, generally heal faster than average thanks to access to magic. Tara and her team got me over another big hump before we left yesterday, but there's still a lot to keep healing.

I should have died a week ago.

And I try to remind myself of that instead of grousing that I want to be ready to gear up and head back out *right now*.

Well, maybe after food. A pang hits my stomach. Definitely after food.

I limp from the room, straightening sweatpants and T-shirt, and scraping grit from my eyes as I go. The compact living room with its beige couch and terrible carpet still has gear stacked through it. It's neat and squared away, like we're out on mission and not on base. Maybe they're ready to head to the barracks rooms in the tower whenever I kick them out. But as much as I prefer my own space, I'm not going to yet.

Kitchen's not much bigger, especially once you add Besim at the round table and Remy cooking at the stove, the narrow counter filled with ingredients.

"I'd ask if we woke you up, but we've been here for forty-five minutes," Bes says. They both have keys, and even if they did need to break in, Remy's the one who warded my apartment. His magic would recognize them both and not attack.

I pull out a chair and join Besim at the table. I don't really have any response since I'm still waking up. He doesn't mind, continuing to tap at the laptop in front of him. He's still in fatigues with long sleeves rolled up to the elbows, chain mail showing. Remy probably ditched his long sleeves and chain mail as soon as they got in the door, switching to a short-sleeved grey ARMY shirt. His inherent fire magic keeps him warm, and he'd probably be in shirtsleeves in the middle of a Detroit winter.

"Cir?" I wince at my gravelly voice.

"Taking a walk." Remy grabs a glass from the cabinet, fills it with water, and sets it on the table.

I frown at him, and he just turns back to the stove. From the sheer amount of stuff on the counter, and probably in the refrigerator decorated with hand-drawn pictures from his son and a few photos of the crew, they must have bought out half the on-base market.

"What do I owe you for all that?" I tip my chin even though his back is turned.

"How long before you kick us out?" he returns.

"Maybe never. Whoever's in the living room is the first line of defense," I reply, and they both chuckle. But it's been too damn quiet in my apartment and in my head for months, and I need it to be the opposite for awhile.

Bes reaches over to the counter's edge and snags a package to set on the table. Thick shortbread squares half dipped in chocolate. Remy's not going to eat them—no chocolate outside emergencies for him—but Bes and I will take care of this entire package before soup if he doesn't stop us.

I drain the water glass, getting myself more before Remy, or Besim, can keep mothering me, and sit back down to start on the cookies. "How long's Cir been gone?"

"Left as soon as we got in." Besim closes his laptop and stacks two cookies on the table in front of him. Cieran trying to outpace whatever his problems are is never really a good sign. Or he's tipping back to a nasty sleep cycle and he's trying to get a head start on being exhausted enough to sleep.

Neither situation bodes well for us and the coming conflict. I can offer to just knock him out with magic. I did one time about six months back, but he ended up sleeping for almost twenty-four hours.

"Day going that well?" I ask.

Remy turns and leans against the counter. "It's hurry up and wait."

Everyone's favorite. I break cookie number two in half and give him the plain side. I probably shouldn't eat so much chocolate. My magic buzzes and hums in response, zipping through my veins faster than normal. But I'd lost it for three months with the stoneheart so don't mind the *feeling* for now.

"We got the all-clear to at least check in with family," Bes says.

Which is probably why they're more relaxed. Usually for me that would mean this—sitting in a room with them trying not to think about Tara or anyone else I've left behind. But now I've got her number in my phone and the comforting feeling of her just out of reach with this heartbond dampener on.

But I'm not sure where my phone is.

"How's Bear?" I ask.

"Mad I can't come home yet." Remy twists enough to grab the canned energy drink behind him. He doesn't drink them often, and it's usually only when he's stressed. There's a few plainclothes monitoring his and Bes's families just in case.

"Sorry." I sweep a few crumbs together with my thumb.

He shrugs like it's no big deal. "I can at least call."

This time Besim and I shoot each other a look. Though Bes's warns me not to blame myself for all this. Bear's been around almost as long as I've known Remy, and if someday I'm half as good a dad as Remy is, I'll be lucky.

The thought stops me in my tracks. I haven't thought about having kids in years, even when Tara and I were together. But back then had been a lot of hiding and lying to each other, and ourselves, while caught in the mess of our families.

Now?

A buzzing noise hits my ear, and Remy crosses over to the counter and grabs my phone from the charger. Either I'd done that hours ago, or one of them had.

He hands it over, and I stare for a moment at Tara's name on the incoming call. It's still hitting odd in my heart, seeing her name and knowing she's back around and doesn't actively hate my guts.

"You gonna answer?" Bes asks mildly.

I narrow my eyes at him and answer. "Hey."

"Hey." Her voice feels like home. Like how it is at Besim's and Remy's houses with their family around. It took me a long time to figure out that their families were normal. Not that I didn't know mine was messed up, but it was almost painful to see so much goodness in one place.

"It is okay that I called? I'm not really sure how to do this." Tara gives a self-conscious laugh.

"It's okay. We just got the all-clear to talk to families," I say.

"Family sounds nice."

I'm almost glad that the stoneheart was active when we met again since now I'm a jumbled mess inside any time I talk to her. And I want to take this dampener off, because talking to her with it on makes it feel like all the years where the bond was gone. Feels a little like those terrifying moments when the sorcerer got hold of the heartbond with his dark magic and started to rip it out.

"How are you feeling?" she asks, not put off by the way I'm pausing between everything. And not just because Besim and Remy are here.

"I'm okay." It's a standard response and one the guys, and very clearly Tara, easily see through. Though she can probably still feel some of the discomfort pressing around me, even with the dampener on and the miles between us.

"Can you flip to video?" she asks.

"You'll have to see Besim and Remy's faces. You sure you want that?" I ask and Tara laughs.

Besim moves the cookies out of my reach in revenge and Remy just smirks, turning back to the stove. I switch the call over to video and tip the phone up against my glass. It takes a second to connect, and when it does, everything's a little fuzzy thanks to Wastelands interference. This probably won't be a long call.

But it's worth it seeing her.

"You look terrible," she says. I crack a smile, mimicking her position and leaning crossed arms on the table.

"I feel a lot better, trust me."

She arches an eyebrow. "Who's more likely to confirm that, Besim or Remy?"

I lift a hand in protest as the others laugh. But, "Besim."

Remy shakes his head and splits another cookie with Besim. He's not denying it though. We'll both cover for each other, unless it's something truly worrying.

"*What* is your shirt, Dej?" she asks. I smirk. It's a pretty dark paramedic joke across the navy fabric. I lean back so she can see the whole thing and she just gives an exasperated smile.

"I probably shouldn't be surprised," she says.

"You shouldn't," Besim chimes in. She smiles again, but it's not hiding the dark circles under her eyes.

"You okay?" I ask, pushing on the muted bond to make sure she won't just avoid the question.

She sighs and props her chin on her hand. "Ish. We've got more soldiers around so it feels safer, but not sleeping very well. I got told I might have to come to Dunhare soon."

I give a sharp glance to the others, but they just shrug. They haven't heard that.

"Who told you that?"

A frown creases between her eyes. "I had to talk to FBI agents. Cason and...starts with an *N*."

"Napier?"

"Yeah." Her face clears, hearing me say the name. But I'm not relieved at all. I want her to stay as far as possible from Damir. I'd been content to stay away from the meetings to sleep, but not anymore. Not if they're trying to pull Tara into potential danger.

"They didn't say when or if I actually am," she tries to reassure, but it's not working.

"Cieran probably knows." I had found some rest, but now I'm back to antsy and it's not just the chocolate. I need him back to get answers.

"Don't bother him," she tries but I arch my eyebrow.

"My job is to bother people."

She laughs, harder when Remy supports with a, "He's very good at it."

"I absolutely believe that." Tara's smirk coaxes one of my own, and warmth fills my chest at the sight of it and the bond strengthening between us for a moment.

Abrupt motion at the door announces Cieran's entry and our attention swings to him. He's got his phone in hand, and grim focus on his face.

"Gear up." He barely stops when he sees me awake. Remy pushes from the counter, arms swinging down by his sides.

"Dej?" Tara whispers, but I can't answer.

"Damir's on the move and he's taken Maya from her apartment." Cir barely gets it out before Besim's chair violently scrapes back from the table. Cieran's hand clamps on Besim's shoulder, somehow keeping the taller soldier in place. "Setanta and Fenrir are on it. Fenrir sent me a location, but that might change in transit. Bes, check her location tag."

The half-troll shoots an angry and almost *helpless* look at Cieran, but our sergeant doesn't back down. "We're going, but we need to know where."

Besim drags his laptop over and starts working, jaw clenched so tight I can almost hear his teeth grinding.

"Rem, go gear up."

Remy turns off the stove and slides around me.

"Cir." Not even Tara's muted protest over the phone stops me from half-rising in my seat. Cieran's sergeant look weighs heavy for the few seconds he assesses.

"You're still injured," he says.

I know it. I know I can't use my bow, can probably only get a few decent swings with the sword. But I can't just let them go. Not if they're about to go face off with Damir.

"I can drive, and I can heal." I know I can do both those things.

"You're hanging back no matter what. Your job is covering Maya if we can get her," Cieran finally says. "Wear as much gear as you can."

Relief sweeps through me, barely quashed by reaching for my phone and finding Tara's wide-eyed disbelief.

"I have to go," I say, recklessly pulling off the dampener bracelet and letting reassurance flow through the bond. It butts up sharply against her fear and worry. *I'll be okay.* We don't have telepathy with our bond, but I push the feeling through.

It takes a second before she nods. "Please be careful."

"I'll call you when I can," I promise and hang up.

Five minutes of muted curses later, I'm in fatigues and boots. I can barely handle the two pounds of the light chain mail under my shirt, I'm not going to be able to wear the twenty-five-pound tac vest with its rune-warded armor plates.

The others stand impatiently as I try to keep from limping too badly from my room and get knives strapped on and my comm hooked in. Remy hands over the medic kit he freed from the underside of my pack. I sling it over my shoulder and take his car keys next.

"I'm feeding everything to your phone," Bes says. His longsword and knives are belted on, and he's got laptop in hand. He's the antsiest of all of us and I don't blame him. If it was Tara out there, I'd be feral by now. I tip my chin up and he gives the same wordless acknowledgment.

He knows I'm not going to let him down.

Cieran looks me over, but before he can change his mind and order me to stay, I grab my keys to lock up. "Let's go."

12

MAYA

THE TWENTY-MINUTE CAR RIDE is marked in absolute silence. Damir makes no move to cross the space I tried to put between us. I'm still pressed up against my door, too distracted by keeping one eye on him to really pay attention to where we're going.

But when we pull to a stop on the outskirts of the southside warehouse district, I feel another tinge of hope. It shouldn't have taken us so long to get here from my apartment. Not if we were taking a direct route. Emmet and Damir don't appear to know this.

Damir slides out, not waiting for Hunnar to get his door. The Shrike doesn't even acknowledge the other elf. Not until someone with the restless energy of a shifter comes out and claims Emmet and Damir's attention.

"Get her inside," Damir throws over his shoulder at Hunnar.

The Nordic elf opens my door and flicks fingers at me. I don't really want to test him, or the others, so I obey. He settles a gentle hand around my upper arm and steers me away from the others.

Six stumbling steps later, once our backs are fully turned, he murmurs in a barely audible voice, "Hit me with whatever you've got and run." His free hand points down the open street in front of us.

I don't stop to question. My hands curl, pulling in as much wild magic as I can until my veins hum, then release it with a few words in ancient Gaelic—*throw, push.*

The spell activates with a percussive blast, hurling him backwards and pushing me into a run in the opposite direction. The reverberations die in my wake, taken over by my pounding feet. I'm just running as fast and as far as I can. But I've never been much of a sprinter or runner.

Shouts rise behind me, driving me on. I tear around a corner, dodging a weed-encrusted bike leaning against a wall. Skid around another corner to the right. I'm not shaking my pursuit, and boots thud louder and louder behind me. There's no place to hide, no narrow alleys or doorways, nothing to duck into. Just long rows of linked townhouses with windows boarded or shattered, weeds overgrowing the sidewalk.

A stitch stabs my left side and I sob for breath. My escape attempt is going to last all of two blocks before they catch me at a walk. I push on, tripping over uneven concrete, barely catching myself on palms and right knee. All points of contact sting as I get upright and keep running.

"Got you!" a rough voice shouts and a desperate scream fights from me as a hand snags my shoulder, jolting it in its socket.

A canine shape launches itself at my attacker with a deep growl. He goes down with a surprised yelp, and I keep running. More shouts rise, and quick rasping steps turn to heavier thudding strides.

The keening whine of an incoming magic strike fills my ears. Hands grab my shoulders and push me down a new street. Muscled bulk pins me to the wall as shrieking cold whips past, some spinning its way around the corner.

It takes a second for my brain to catch up and start slamming my fist into this new attacker's chest, calling up another spell to throw him across the street.

"Hey, Artemis, Artemis!" a deep voice cuts through my panic. It's the safe word. I stop long enough to look at him. Lean, angular features shadowed in scruff. Ratty clothes and jacket that smell unpleasantly like the river docks.

My mind screeches and skids. Wolfhound at the apartment. Something attacking the men. Stranger helping me.

"Fates, I hope your name isn't Charming," the stupid statement bursts from me.

A smile slashes his face, turning him into something less frightening. "No, Tommy just thinks he's hilarious."

Without time to question, he gets a hand on my upper back and pushes me forward. "Keep moving."

The contact doesn't let up as he takes us through a side door, winding through a darkened interior filled with dust and rot and shattered glass. Out another door into the blinding sunlight. Across another street with similarly abandoned buildings and through a narrow alley.

Shouts echo behind us. A howl rises up and his face twists in annoyance. A beat-up green Explorer screeches to a halt at the alley exit, blocking us off. I balk, but he keeps pushing me forward.

"Hey!" A figure in grey fatigues comes around the car, a glint of steel in his hand. I slam to a halt as I recognize Dejan. He's poised to fight, knife held in a reverse grip. My rescuer doesn't flinch, just pushes me again.

Dejan's posture doesn't relax, not until the shifter uses the password again. "Artemis."

The elf lowers his arm, nodding to the shifter, then looking to me. "Get in the car."

This is the second time I've been told that today but this time I think I'll trust the person saying it. Given that he looks *terrible* and he and his cousin are clearly no fans of each other.

I'm halfway into the car when I focus on the shifter again. Barking has started up and is getting closer. "Will you be okay?"

He flashes another smile, dangerous this time. "Don't worry about me."

Dejan slams his door shut and I do the same, twisting to watch the shifter break into a run, heading away from us as we peel out. I blink and a grey wolfhound has taken his place just before it vanishes around the corner.

"You okay?" Dejan's voice jerks my attention to him. I brace against the seat as he takes a turn faster than I'm comfortable with. I grab for my seatbelt. Halt in the middle of buckling as I catch sight of his phone in the cupholder. It's got a red dot hovering on a street view, and it's moving along in time with the car.

"Is that *me*?"

He skirts another corner and we're on a busier street. "Technically it's your phone."

I slam the buckle in place and grab my phone from my back pocket like it can give me answers. "How did you...?"

Dejan checks the rearview and side mirrors, slides into a new lane, and takes another turn. "This seems like a conversation for Besim."

"Besim...?" My mouth works.

"Are you okay?" he asks again.

"Are you guys tracking me?" My voice raises a notch. Gratitude that they found me this way mixes with disbelief.

"I'm going to take that as a yes, you're okay." He changes lanes again, this time to get onto the main highway around town. After another glance in mirrors, he's apparently satisfied and leans back against the driver's seat. "By the way, you need to turn that off. Chucking it out the window is preferable."

"What?"

"That's a *firren* beacon for more than just us. Turn it off or break it."

I keep staring at him, clutching my phone. He reaches over and plucks it from my hands. I'm ready to lunge across the seat to punch him if he tries to throw it. But he jams a thumb against the power button and it shuts off. The red blip on his screen disappears in tandem. He hands the phone back.

I slump back against my seat, hands pressing the device against my stomach. It takes another few seconds before shakiness hits. The phone slides into my lap, tremoring hands clutching each other. I fold forward, lips clamping shut against threatening sobs. My eyes squeeze shut, but it only helps me see the frantic minutes of escape again.

"Hey, you okay?" Dejan's gentle voice slides through the panic. It's so different from his cousin, but still holds some of the same inflections. I shake my head.

"Can I put my hand on your shoulder?" he asks. I'm still folded over, my head brushing the glove compartment. I get full view of ripped jeans and bloody knee from where I fell.

I nod in answer, a little shocked at myself for allowing another Kostic this close. I've been around Dejan for nine months, and still "known" seems like a strong word. But he's always been decent.

His hand settles on my shoulder, and the warmth of elvish healing magic spreads. It slows my heart rate, and it's like I can feel it shooing some of the adrenaline away. Light stinging hits my palms and knee and when I unfold to better look at my palms, only traces of blood remain.

The contact lets up. I draw a steadier breath and straighten. He winces a little as he settles his hand back on the wheel.

"Thanks," I murmur. Dejan nods in return, focused on the road.

"Where's Besim?" I ask. A faint quirk hits his cheek. I'm not sure what's so funny.

"Hopefully kicking some ass with the others. I got to be getaway driver." Dejan checks the mirrors again. "But I know he's just as anxious to see you."

Heat rushes to my face at the light tone. "Will they be okay?"

His bruised jaw works for a second. "Yeah." It's clear he wishes he was with them, and it's evident why he's not.

"You look terrible." A reddish scar runs across his cheek, another at his hairline. The bruising, plus the way he's now got his left elbow propped against the window and tilting that way ever so slightly.

"I wish I could say you should see the other guy."

My focus dips to my hands again and I pick some of the dried blood off my palm. "I think I have."

Dejan's sharp chuckle slashes between us. "Yeah. Family, right?" he finishes wryly.

Some sort of desperate excuse for a laugh comes from me. I scrub the backs of my fingers under my eye. "I'm really sorry."

He changes lanes and exits off the highway. "If we're all apologizing, it's my family who got yours into this crap."

I study him again. He doesn't have a Shrike tattoo on his neck, but there's some skilled elf and fae tattoo removal artists out there. He's never been especially *friendly*. At least to me, but turns out we were hiding the same secrets about our pasts in Detroit.

"You're really a Kostic?" I ask as the car slows to a stop.

He's silent as he waits for the light to change, thumb tapping against the wheel. "Really a Kostic or really a Shrike?"

My shoulders lift. "Both?"

Dejan inclines his head in understanding. "Kostic by birth. My dad was training me to take over the Shrikes one day, but..." He shrugs. "One day I decided to use my access to gather a couple hard drives of information and pass it to the Feds. Then hightailed it out of Detroit and never looked back."

I recognize where we are, and we're a few streets away from the Army base. I relax a tiny fraction. "I can see why your cousin doesn't like you."

"Ah," he makes a dismissive sound. "He's always been an asshole."

A small laugh jolts from me. If you'd told me a week ago that I'd share a car with two Detroit Kostics, I'd have laughed to cover a shudder and tried to lightly say the truth. That would be my worst nightmare.

But the Kostic rolling down his window and presenting credentials to the base gate guard and giving some explanation for me is so completely different from Damir that it's hard to believe Dejan was ever part of the same organization.

We pull through the gate and he navigates to the Drax Guard tower I've been in once. After the incident with Damien Janvier, Nadi and I had to come and give our version of events to the commander. I'd hoped I wouldn't have to come back. Other than maybe just a visit. But here I am.

Dejan parks, but doesn't make a move to get out once he shuts the car off. There's some hesitation about him when he looks to me and asks, "We good?"

No blame or anger or hard feelings for each other's families and the way it's turning into one giant mess invading lives and the families we actually want.

"We're good," I affirm. He cracks a smile, filled with the same threads of relief that peter through me.

"You ever miss Detroit?" I ask suddenly. I don't know if he even wants to talk about it, but now that I'm not avoiding mention of the city, having someone to talk about the parts I loved might be nice.

"Yeah, sometimes," he says, the same smile crooking the corner of his mouth. He shakes his head. "Not winters though."

"Oh hell no," I firmly agree. Oregon winters, at least around Dunhare, are much milder and shorter without the frigid addition of winds off the lake.

Dejan chuckles and I relax a little more. It's nice to finally not to be subconsciously on guard around him.

"Let's head inside," he says.

"What about the others?" Worry flares up from where it had been lurking for a few moments in the background.

He pushes open his door and pockets the keys. "They'll be here when they get here."

I frown and get out. My expression deepens at the way he's obviously limping on the way to the door. I don't really want to know what happened to him.

"That's not reassuring." I hasten to his side, not sure if he needs, or wants, help from me.

"Welcome to the Army. It's hurry up and wait."

13

Maya

A FAINT CHILL GREETS us in the wide atrium. I like the heptagonal shape, the columns at each point stretching up three floors. It gives it an open feel, and automatically draws attention up to the A.S.A. flag hanging opposite the main door. Blue fields are divided by three off-center stripes. Red and white alternate, and stars pepper the blue. To the right is the Army flag, and to the left is the Drax Guard. A red fire drake coils around a blood-coated sword. It's just as ferocious as the motto.

Dejan appears to be waiting in the lobby for something, hand tapping the comm in his ear. I sidle off, curious about the rest of the building and the way it's built. An assignment earlier this semester had us going to older buildings and writing reports on architecture and what magic we could identify before comparing it to plans from the city archives.

The entire southwest wall holds an extra silence. A slab of granite rises above me, names etched into the polished surface. I skim over them, drawn to another reminder at the top—*Fear No Fire.*

I turn from the names to the pictures. Some are old, starting to brown at the edges. Some are formal portraits of solemn-faced men staring out in uniform, an A.S.A. flag behind them. Then there's smaller pictures, most taped to the fringes of the wall. Groups of men in fatigues and armor, some single shots, all over the world, mostly involving laughter and it seems, in many cases, something stupid.

My eye catches a familiar face and I pause. It's Cieran. Even from his profile, I recognize the backward hat, the sunglasses, the head tipped back in laughter as another guy holds something in a pair of tongs, offering it to an elf of Arabic heritage. The elf wears a crown that looks like it's made of candy wrappers. They're in fatigues, somewhere dusty and rocky. A smile rises to my lips. The picture next to it includes a half-fae who must have been taking the first. The four of them stand in a line, weapons and armor on, smiles in place. It takes a second to realize, and when I do, emotion hits the back of my nose and stings my eyes.

This is a memorial wall and Cieran's crew is Besim, Remy, and Dejan.

I quickly scrub at my nose and step back. Dejan's a few feet away, attention focused on the wall as well. He probably knows some of the men.

"Sorry." I retreat a little further. It feels like I just intruded on something that isn't meant for me to see.

He reaches out and pushes down the corner of some peeling tape that holds a picture of two soldiers, arms slung around each other's necks, one laughing, one rowdily singing into a rolled-up piece of paper.

"It's a memorial wall. It's meant to bring some part of them back when you look," he says.

My hands curl around my upper arms for a moment before I free one long enough to point at the picture with Cieran. "Who are they?"

Dejan tilts his chin at the wall. "Moreno, Nazari, Anderson."

I find the names, and trace to the dates off to the right side. Just over two years ago. There's only one name under theirs. Six months ago.

"Killed in action?" I ask, though it's obvious this wall is not for every member of the Guard who served in the last two hundred years.

"Yeah." His hands slide into the pockets of his trousers. I wonder who mimicked who with that posture—Damir or Dejan. But it seems more comfortable on Dejan.

"How do you do it?" I blurt. Looking at this wall...what if this is Besim one day? What if this is Dejan or Remy or Cieran, and Bes is the one left behind just staring at this wall? How do they go out time after time when this could be all that was left of them? And could I be strong enough to wait for him to come back?

"You do it for the man next to you. You do it for the people you leave behind. You do it because no one else is *firren* going to," Dejan says. "You do it because you want to try to leave the world a slightly better place and you're the kind of person who can get their hands dirty cleaning out the crap."

It's low, honest. And the look he gives me is almost daring. Am I going to run from that? From him? From Besim? Am I strong enough to wait for Besim to come back?

I don't know. Because I don't know if I'll stick around long enough to see. My family brought trouble to their door and if any of them, or Nadi, gets hurt because of it, I don't know what I'll do.

"You won't find better than Besim." It's like Dejan is reading my mind. My cheeks heat and I glance at him. I'm starting to think that elves really can hear heartbeat changes. Or maybe it is just obvious that I really like Besim Antilles.

Still, it's nice to know that I'd have the approval of Dejan, who always seemed like the hardest to get.

"Corporal." A new voice sends Dejan flinching.

"*Fir*, Eckhart!" He jolts away, exposing a younger soldier with an expression rather like a satisfied cat. "Wear a bell, for Fates' sake."

Eckhart only flashes another grin. "Wolfe got trapped by the agents just now, but he'll want a report ASAP." His glance settles on me. It makes me feel like I'm in trouble. "While he's finishing up with them, quartermaster is probably going to be the best bet to help find Ms. Lyons some temporary lodging on base."

"On base?" Now I'm startled into motion, looking at both of them, unsure if this is some new threat or not.

Eckhart gives me a tight, sympathetic smile. "At least until we determine what the threat is to you, and if it's safe for you to go home."

A shiver races down my arms. I don't want to go home. Not with the fresh memory of Damir Kostic strolling in after *my brother* let him in. I mutely nod and feel a little better as Dejan tilts his chin up, sharp green eyes locked on to me with what feels like a promise of protection. And I get why Besim trusts the elf.

"I was going to stop by anyway and see if Myerson had any pain meds," Dejan says.

I eye him and the way he's almost completely shifted his weight off one leg. "Should you be in hospital?" I ask.

"Yeah, actually," Dejan replies easily.

"Be up in fifteen," Eckhart says and vanishes.

I nod uselessly and let Dejan lead the way deeper into the building. It starts to abruptly sink in. Basically being kidnapped from my apartment, getting rescued, and now existing in some sort of protective custody on the Army base for Fates know how long. It's becoming a churning, writhing mess right behind my breastbone, clamoring to get out. I'm not sure if I'm going to sit down and ugly cry or stand there and *scream*.

So when we barely step out of the atrium and there's quick boot steps and a "*Maya!*" I lunge to meet Besim, wrapping my arms around him and his armor. His arms circle me, gently tucking me close. Even though my forehead is pressed against a tac vest, it's the safest I've felt in a long time.

"You okay?" Tears threaten again at his low voice humming just above my head.

"Yeah." My voice cracks a little and his hold tightens in response. The *this seems like a question for Besim* pops back in my head and I yank away and punch his arm. And immediately regret it.

"Ow!" I shake my stinging knuckles. "You couldn't have not done the stoneskin thing?" I scowl.

He looks so dorkily apologetic as he lifts a hand. "Chain mail," he says.

I glare, rubbing my aching fist, before smacking his upper arm much more lightly with open palm. "Nerd stuff?" I punch again. "You used my location and you didn't tell me?"

Chagrin softens his face again and his shoulders slump. "Sorry. I was hoping we wouldn't need it. I just...didn't want you to panic over anything else. But it's weirder not to tell you."

I prop my hands on my hips. It's hard to be mad when he's genuinely remorseful.

"Well...extenuating circumstances being what they are," I start and a slight smile cracks his features. It sets my heart to skipping again.

"Do you still have your phone?" he asks.

"I turned it off," I say. "*Someone* wanted to throw it out the window at seventy miles per hour." I turn to glare at Dejan who doesn't look the least sorry.

"Technically *I* turned it off. I listen sometimes," he tells Besim.

The half-troll shakes his head. "One time apparently."

Dejan ignores him with a slightly injured look that fades just as fast as it appeared. "What are you here for?"

"Equipment and a new crew. We're setting up some surveillance for now," Besim says. "And Cieran says that if Wolfe doesn't ground you, he is."

Dejan mutters something in elvish that doesn't sound extremely complimentary of his commanding officers.

"That's probably what he said you'd say." Besim shakes his head.

"I can give you a more specific message." Dejan smirks, and a laugh teases my chest.

"No thanks." Besim gently shoves his shoulder before focusing on me again. "You sure you're okay?"

I nod, more than halfway wanting to step back into his arms, tac vest and all. But he's on mission and already putting space between us on the way to his next stop. Maybe we are just friends in his eyes.

"Take care of her." The way he looks at Dejan and the slightly deeper tone has me doubting that. As does the look he gives me right after. Like he's afraid I might vanish right then and there. My heart dips to my toes then soars back up so quick it leaves me breathless.

"Besim..." I'm halfway to him before I register that I've moved. He leans toward me, head tipping down. I tear my focus from his lips and up to his eyes. "Be careful."

He doesn't reply, just nods after a few eternal heartbeats, then strides away. I don't know what we are, but I know that part of my heart belongs to Besim Antilles, whether he knows it or not. And I'll wait for as long as it takes for him to come back.

14

BESIM

WALKING AWAY IN THIS moment is one of the hardest things I've ever done. I hadn't been ready for the crushing relief at seeing Maya safe. Or the way it felt right to hold her.

I'm sure the way I feel about her is splayed all over my face. That look she gave me promises that she doesn't see me just as a friend. But I get Remy's hesitation now. It seems dangerous to keep waiting to ask, but there's not really time for a "do you want to go out with me?" conversation when I need to grab equipment and get back across town so Remy and I can set up surveillance. I'd prefer both her and the team to be safe and not in the middle of mission before we have that conversation.

I'm halfway to the quartermaster's hall when Remy's quiet voice crackles through the comms. "Bes, get up to the CO's office now."

I freeze mid-stride, hearing the unmistakable sounds of a ticked-off Cieran in the background. "What happened?"

"FBI," Rem says wryly. "They're trying to get us to pull back. Cieran's pissed."

I pivot and head for the stairs instead, taking them two at a time to the fourth floor. Cieran's not the only one. We have the Shrikes' location and need to recon so we can hit it and just be done with this.

Wolfe's door is open and voices overlap. I get there in seconds. Agents Napier and Cason both scowl at me. Napier points back out the door, like he can shoo me away. I ignore him. Eckhart's braced with arms across his chest to my right and he makes no move to usher me away either.

Wolfe paces behind his desk, phone to his ear. Attempting to talk Cieran down. From the deepening annoyance on Napier's face, his fae hearing can pick up Cieran's multiple expletives just fine through the line. Or maybe through my comm.

"Sergeant," Wolfe finally says in the crisp commanding officer *"you're done"* voice. I can picture the mulish expression on Cieran's face like he's in front of me. Remy's faint scoff crackles through the comm.

"You're on speaker." And there's a very clear *don't* in Wolfe's tone.

CO sets the phone down and switches it to speaker. I'm miles away but I can *feel* Cieran seething. Could just be me too at the light of faint triumph in both agents' faces.

"Sergeant," Napier starts.

"Cir," Remy mutters in warning and I tap my comm to send the same burst back through the connection.

"Agent," Cieran spits back. Wolfe's eyes shutter towards resignation. Or commiseration. It's hard to tell with him sometimes.

Napier sets hands against the desk, leaning forward to better project to the phone. "The Bureau has lead in this case. You will stand down and return to base."

"I'm looking right at the Shrikes' *firren* base of operations. We can get intel right now," Cieran replies in measured anger.

Cason angles closer. "What about the deep cover agents? What if you blow their cover?"

"I'm not going to be walking down the street in full *firren* armor asking them nicely to *fir* off."

"Sergeant." Napier's fingers press against the desk. "You're risking blowing this entire operation. Pull back. We'll use surveillance from our team already in place."

Even Wolfe shifts slightly at that. The same frustration fills me. What do they think we do in the Guard? Just smash and grab?

"What if I don't trust *your* team?" Cieran asks, voice dangerously even.

Napier straightens, face creasing past annoyance and toward anger. "Return to base. That's an order," the agent says.

Wolfe's sharp glance and intended words are cut off by Cieran's "You don't get to *firren* order me, you—"

Abrupt silence falls along with a telltale ringing whine that's Remy using magic to shut the sergeant up before he says something he'll actually regret. Napier gives a mirthless smile at the phone. Wolfe scoops it up, switching back to just him and Cieran.

"I *am* ordering, Sergeant," Wolfe says evenly. "Back to base and to my office."

The "yes, sir," is frigid and Wolfe takes another second to set the phone down. But before he can say anything, Napier props hands on his hips.

"Are all your soldiers so insubordinate, Captain?" he asks with a sideways glance at me.

"My soldiers don't answer to you," Wolfe replies. He doesn't have magic but the temperature in the room drops twenty degrees. Eckhart prowls closer to the desk, body tensed like he's in mountain cougar form and about to jump. Some slight wariness slants across Napier's features. He's got magic, but he must finally remember that soldiers, and especially the Drax Guard, are trained to fight against wielders.

"I'd appreciate my case not being blown by soldiers ready to charge," the fae says. "That attempt to grab Lyons was already disruptive enough."

"The successful rescue?" Wolfe barely beats me to it.

Napier smiles thinly. "Luck."

Eckhart's vibrating now, discomfiting stare boring into the agents. My hand clenches around my longsword.

"We don't believe in luck," I say. I brace for the reprimand or the whiplash of Napier suddenly becoming "good cop" again, but neither comes.

"I want a debrief with Lyons and your other man. And I don't want to see O'Donnell until he cools off." Napier retreats from the office, Cason in tow.

It takes a few seconds for all three of us to get closer to calm.

"Door," Wolfe snaps. I don't take it personally, twisting to knock the door closed. He jams a hand through his short hair before abruptly becoming more calm. The CO tugs at the bottom of his shirt and at the sleeve cuffs, returning to unflappable before my eyes.

"Tell Kalama 'good catch.'" Wolfe indicates my comm. I offer a faint smile and do as ordered. Remy huffs back.

"Put me on," Remy says. I take the earpiece out and turn up the volume as I close the gap between me and the desk. "Thank you, sir." There's a tinny edge to his voice. "Sarge is cooling off for a second," he continues.

"I want as much information as you can get on the way out," Wolfe says.

"Yes, sir."

"I'm routing a pick up for you. They'll be there in fifteen minutes, and you and Cieran will get in."

Remy affirms. Guess I'm staying here, then. Wolfe flicks his hand, and I return the volume to normal and refix the earpiece.

"Antilles." Wolfe props hands on his hips. "Get Kostic up here before the agents find him and the entire base implodes."

A chuckle bursts from me before I can stop it. "Yes, sir."

The corner of Wolfe's mouth twitches. "Eckhart, go tail our friends and bring them up here in ten minutes."

His aide allows the same flicker of amusement. He's been around Wolfe too long. "Yes, sir."

Eckhart moves around me with barely a sound as I pull out my phone and call Dejan. He wasn't popping into the comms conversation, so he's lurking somewhere. Or managed to make himself feel worse with the sudden activity and doesn't want us to know.

I'm praying it's not the second as he picks up.

"Miss me already?" he asks. Faint strain edges his voice.

"What did you do?" I ask, head shaking slightly.

"Why are you assuming—?" Dejan's cut off by an annoyed sound and then Maya's clear voice, "He just sat down really sudden and has been cursing a lot."

I rub my temple and sigh. "Where are you two?"

"We made it to the quartermaster, I think. She left to get something for him."

"I'm fine," Dejan complains in the background, but there's another frustrated curse.

"Okay, I'll be down there in a second," I say and hang up. Wolfe has hands on hips, mouth in a line. I just shrug.

He shakes his head. "Medics make the worst patients. Bully him right back."

I chuckle. "Yes, sir."

15

Besim

I MAKE IT TO the quartermaster's hall in minutes. There's another soldier running inventory on the wall shelving. I don't wait for him to turn around and let me in, so I vault the countertop instead. He turns with a quick complaint that dies when he sees it's me.

I quickly wave and he frowns in response, an eyebrow quirk warning me to never do that again. Dejan's complaints guide me through the door to the main supply aisles. He sits on a bench, hand pressed against his leg. Quartermaster Emma Myerson has hands on hips, lecturing him. The dwarf doesn't take crap from anyone, especially those who come back with ruined equipment. Maya stands across from them, concern warring with amusement at watching the elf and dwarf trade annoyed words.

Maya glances up at me as I go to stand next to her. "Is he always like this?" she asks.

"Worse." My smile widens with her chuckle. Dejan breaks off to glare at me, but the expression holds no vitriol.

"Antilles." Emma throws up her hands in surrender. "He's all yours."

But she rests her hand on Dejan's forearm and the elf nods back in reassurance. She leaves us with a stock of chocolate and a med kit on the bench beside Dejan.

I crouch next to him as he releases his leg and starts digging through the bag. "What do you need?"

"A new skeleton." He winces as he gets a bottle of meds out and takes two pills. I don't miss the tremor in his hand as he unbuttons his fatigues shirt and shrugs out of it. He takes a short breath and goes for the chain mail. I help him get it over his head and set it to the side. His long-sleeved shirt underneath is spotted with sweat.

Dejan ignores my look and pulls it up to check a bandage on his ribs. A sound comes from Maya and I glance to her. She stares in horror at the bruising still covering Dejan. Most of the magic went to healing his countless internal injuries. Another week with the doctors and he'd have been better off, but here we are instead.

"You were going to try to fight someone like *that*?" she asks. Dejan flicks a look up at her before pressing his green-tinted hand to the site, channeling his own healing magic to it. He eases a relieved breath.

"Can you get the charm kit out?" he asks.

I reach across him and snag the med bag, rifling through until I pull out the zippered pouch that holds small patches pre-prepped with healing charms to help a medic spread out their magic. He takes the patch I open and presses it to the side of his neck over the largest blood vessel, sending the magic right into his bloodstream.

His eyes close and he slouches further against the wall, the tightness finally easing from his face. I nudge his arm, and he cracks open one eye. "Don't tell Cir."

"We need to check your vision if you think I'm Remy," I say. Ironically, between the two of us, Remy is the one who can't tell a lie.

He opens his other eye and his lips thrum in a sigh. "One thing to know about Besim," he says conversationally to Maya. I brace. "He's a snitch."

I shake my head as she chuckles. Dejan tilts a smile and points to the charm kit. I get him another one. He tosses the used patch on the bench and presses the fresh one to his neck. Green tinges his fingers with an accompanying wince as the bruising on his face and around his eye turn two shades lighter. I flick the back of his hand in a warning not to keep being stupid and he just lifts his middle finger from the patch in response.

"See?" I tell Maya. "Worse."

I tuck the kit back into the bag and nudge Dejan's knee.

"I'm fine, Mom," he grouses.

"What did we say about emotional honesty?" I barely get it out evenly.

He shakes his head around his grin. "You're so stupid."

I push back to my feet, taking the used patch from him as I go. "And annoying, and right all the time. Stop being so disgustingly emotional. It's embarrassing for you, honestly."

Dejan chuckles, head still tipped back against the wall. "Shouldn't you be getting gear and leaving?"

"Change of plans." I sneak a glance at Maya as she edges closer.

"What happened?" Dejan's voice lowers dangerously.

"The FBI," I say wryly. His scowl deepens as I update him on the last few minutes. "Come on." I snag his shoulder. "CO wants us back in his office."

"I didn't do anything this time." Dejan smirks faintly as he gets to his feet with my help. He balances more evenly between his feet now.

"Give yourself five minutes." I roll my eyes. He chuckles as he gets chain mail and shirt back on.

"You need anything?" I ask Maya. There's some blood staining her jeans but no apparent injury.

She tucks arms across her stomach, but her smile is freer than earlier today outside the coffee shop. Saints, that feels like *days* ago, not hours. "I won't turn down some emotional support chocolate."

Dejan scoops up one of the bars from the bench and tosses it to her. "If that's not enough, Besim gives really good hugs."

Maya's eyes go wide, and she looks at me in the same horrified embarrassment hitting me. Dejan snickers. At least until I reach out to grab him in a retaliatory hug. He ducks around me with a few elvish words and another laugh.

"Emma, I love you dearly!" he calls.

"*Fir* off, Kostic!" she calls from somewhere in the back.

He sticks the other chocolate bar in his thigh pocket. "I'm going to piss off some FBI agents. You coming?" He spins and makes for the door.

I flip the comms back to two-way. "Remy, what's your status? Your worse half is being an absolute gremlin."

Remy's laugh is echoed by Dejan as he ducks out of the door. I sigh and look to Maya who's trying not to laugh as she turns the chocolate bar in her hands.

"Sure you don't need anything?" I ask.

She fiddles with the wrapper, then tilts a shy look up at me. "I honestly wouldn't turn down another hug."

Ignoring the way my heart flips, I lift one arm, intending just to loop it around her shoulders. But she wraps her arms around me, resting her head against my chest. A breath shudders through her and my hold tightens in response.

"Thanks for coming after me," she murmurs. "Even if you were spying on my phone." Maya tips her head up against my vest to show one twinkling eye.

"I'm really sorry," I halfway protest. She leans against me for a second before pulling back abruptly, scrubbing her hand under her nose.

"Maya," I start, unsure what I'm going to say, but needing to say *something*. Maya stills, then steps back, looking up at me with forced brightness.

"Don't we need to be following Dejan?"

It kills any sort of fumbling attempt at confession, and leaves an odd knot in my chest. Whatever we are, maybe she doesn't want it. I manage to smile back. "Yeah."

When we make it out to the hallway, through the counter access door this time, Dejan is waiting for us. He leans against the wall, hands in his pockets. A teasing smirk fades as he studies the way Maya and I are a few feet apart. A question lingers in the slight tilt of his head but my lips flatten back. I'm not really sure what happened. Not sure what's going on since she's not looking at me, focused on minutely adjusting the slight bend to the wrapper corner.

"Elevator." I point him down the hall, fighting a wince at how strained my voice sounds. Dejan graciously doesn't let his face say anything about it, just leads the way to the elevator and back to Wolfe's office where the FBI already await us.

16

MAYA

THE ELEVATOR RIDE AND short walk to Wolfe's office is quiet. My focus stays on the chocolate bar I've yet to eat. Dejan's look to Besim in the hall had been just as painfully obvious as the confusion in Besim's eyes when I'd stepped away.

I'm tired of the ebb and flow of intense emotion that've been nonstop hitting for the last few hours. Though this last dose was my fault. I was the one who stupidly asked for the hug, putting myself back in his arms before my brain caught up and reminded me that distance was best.

I might not do better than Besim Antilles, but he can do a lot better than me.

We arrive at the commander's office and Dejan and Besim stand rigid and tense even after permission to stand at ease. They angle around me like they're protecting me from the FBI agents once I'm introduced.

Tension stretches across this office like suspension bridge cables. I don't like being part of it. The soldiers don't move, Wolfe stays behind his desk, and the rangy shifter who'd come for us in the lobby is just off to my right side, arms crossed and expression much too neutral.

I go through the events again and again, from Emmet showing up in my apartment, to clambering in the car with Dejan. Agents Napier and Cason ask questions, slightly rephrased from the previous, like they're trying to get me to slip up or uncover some information I don't even know I have.

My mouth is parched and my feet ache by the time they appear to start being satisfied. Dejan's given a few answers in a tone that's so far from the friendly way we'd talked and he'd joked around with Besim. He's always been abrupt, but the way he interacts with the agents might as well be in a new hemisphere of cold.

"Are these Good Samaritans or agents of yours?" Cason asks Wolfe. Another cable gets added to the tension, winched tight enough to snap.

"Are you always in the habit of unearthing any undercover agent in the vicinity?" Wolfe asks.

"No, I'm just interested in finding potential weak links in criminal organizations," Cason replies.

I'd hesitated to give much information. Years of living in Detroit and dealing with cops of varying degrees of straight has a lot of people less inclined to be completely forthcoming. And now it feels like I did something wrong in even giving the indication that some of the men helped in my escape.

Besim has the same focused glare at the agents. Until I reach out and lightly touch his forearm. I shouldn't, but I need someone to help me navigate this. The same confusion mixed with a little hurt still lingers in the corners of his eyes. I definitely didn't think this through since I got his attention with no way to audibly ask my question. Maybe some of my desperation sneaks through anyway, or more likely, he's just really good at reading me. But he gives a slight shake of his head and a quick sideways glance to the agents. Don't say much more. Got it.

"We have surveillance footage from our teams. We'll have some images pulled for Miss Lyons to confirm later," Napier interrupts. Cason subsides, but the look he gives Napier promises they're talking about this later. Which is interesting, since the fae was introduced as lead agent.

An abrupt knock sends Eckhart around us, opening the door to admit Cieran and Remy.

They both salute and immediately slant into easier positions when Wolfe waves his hand. Cieran grabs the collar of his tac vest, and Remy leans back against the doorframe, arms tucked across his chest. The warlock immediately looks to Dejan and the elf juts his chin up. Remy arches an eyebrow and checks wordlessly with Besim, who gives a slight shake of his head. A faint smile twitches in the corner of Remy's mouth in response.

It makes my own smile threaten, watching this wordless exchange. My attention is quickly drawn back to the office, where Cieran has introduced a few counter-cables just by walking in. All feelings aside, I'm using Besim as a shield when everything snaps and starts collapsing.

He must sense this and angles a look down at me, one eyebrow raised. I don't have his team's effortless wordless communication down, so I just look away.

"We need access to the surveillance footage," Cieran says, and Cason leans forward, prepped to argue. I want to warn him not to since I don't think arguing with Cieran O'Donnell will lead to anything good. But Napier holds out a hand between the two men and they both throw a glare toward each other.

"You'll get it, Sergeant."

All four soldiers twitch at the soothing tone. Dejan shakes his head in sharp annoyance.

"In exchange, I want all reports sent to me immediately." Napier directs this at Wolfe.

The captain thinks it over with no change to his stoic expression. Then, "Done."

"And Maya Lyons goes into protective custody," Cason announces.

That gets a bigger reaction than the borderline crisis negotiation over surveillance footage. I'm not the only one protesting. Besim leans toward me, and I close the distance. I don't want to go anywhere else.

"I..." I quickly get talked over.

"This base has too many ingress points. It's too dangerous for her to stay here," Cason says. "We've got plenty of high security locations she can stay."

"And who's watching her?" Cieran asks.

"We'll have a team of highly trained agents on her," Cason replies almost condescendingly. Cieran visibly bristles, but Wolfe interjects.

"I agree with getting her somewhere safe."

I want to protest, and some faint rumble comes from Besim where I'm almost tucked up against his side. I need to step away, but I'm suddenly terrified that they'll take me away right *now* and it'll be the last time I'll see Besim.

"We'll get things prepped and come pick her up tomorrow," Napier announces. That seems like a truce and a relieved exhale slithers between my lips. Besim's hand falls back to his side. I hadn't even noticed that his arm had been positioned low in front of me.

The agents take their leave, and Remy barely moves out of their way. Wolfe sighs and props hands on hips. He mutters something in an unfamiliar language, and Cieran smiles mirthlessly.

"Okay. Miss Lyons, you'll stay on base for tonight. Quartermaster Myerson is already getting something prepped for you and there will be a guard on the house." Wolfe glances up at all of us, lingering longer on

Besim. "She'll send the details to you, Sergeant. In the meantime." Wolfe glances at me almost wryly. "You'll stay with Crew Six. My apologies."

I smile faintly. "Thank you, Captain."

"All of you are dismissed and I don't want to see any of you for at least an hour. Preferably not until tomorrow." Wolfe looks one breath short of grabbing a stiff drink, and I don't blame him.

Remy stands fully aside and waves for me to go first. I wait in the hall for all of them. I look at the chocolate bar, half-melted and forgotten in my hand. Hopefully wherever we're going has a refrigerator I can stick this in and eat later. Emotional support snacks are definitely still a need.

"Well." Dejan sticks hands in his pockets. "Bes, you inviting her over for dinner?"

17

Besim

So Maya's coming for dinner. Remy and Dejan beat us back to the apartment after Remy bullied Dejan back into the car to drive him the few blocks home. Maya didn't say much as she walked with Cieran and me. Once we're inside and she sheepishly asks if she can stick the chocolate in the fridge, she heads to the bathroom.

And I get pinned by three looks as we stand in Dejan's kitchen.

"What did you say?" Dejan keeps his voice low. He and Remy both stand by the stove. It took two seconds of being inside for Remy to ditch half his armor and get back to work on the soup that probably had barely cooled in the bare two hours we were gone.

"Nothing!" I protest in a muted tone.

Cieran leans against the short counter opposite the stove, hands back around his tac vest collar. "What happened?" He keeps the same whisper.

I shrug. I'm still not sure what exactly happened in that moment where she stepped away with an expression of barely shrouded misery.

"You need to talk to her."

I level a stare at Dejan. "You've had a girlfriend again for a week and suddenly you're the expert?"

He smirks and Cieran gives a low chuckle. "He's right though," the sergeant says.

I send another glare around the kitchen. They are right, and usually I'm the one promoting open communication, but I'm just not sure what to do, or how it'll help.

Remy watches me for a second, then digs out his phone. He gives me a pointed look as he taps the screen and puts it to his ear.

"Oh shit," Cieran remarks. Dejan tilts a glance at Remy, somewhere between amused and proud. I'm somewhat less amused, even if I'm also happy he's finally calling Sara.

"Hey," Remy says. His focus falls to where he's scuffing a boot against the ground. "Do you want to go out with me?"

A smile breaks across his face. "Yeah, a date." He chuckles. "Yes, just the two of us." He flicks a glance at Cieran. "Technically yes, we're on mission. I don't know, next Friday?" Another grin bordering on dorky. "Okay. See you later."

He hangs up and returns his phone to the pocket.

"Well, damn," Cieran says. "We've got to finish this by next Friday. Remy's got a date."

I shake my head, fighting a smile as Dejan drops a hand on Remy's shoulder and jostles him.

"I still get to say 'it's about time,'" I tell the warlock. Remy just chuckles.

"Really have no excuse now," Cieran tells me.

"Wait," Dejan says. "Is this what it's like for Bes all the time?"

Remy smirks. "I think we need to soak in this moment."

Cieran chuckles, falling into step with them. I shake my head, fighting another smile though I can't really be annoyed to get a taste of my own medicine. Especially as all three say in low unison, "Talk to her, Bes."

I almost break my no-cursing habit to more silently flip them off. Especially as the bathroom door clicks and Maya steps back out. Remy shoos us out of the tiny area so he can finish dinner.

Cieran and I start taking off vests and weapons in the living room. Dejan gets water for Maya and she slowly comes into the living room as the elf stays behind and starts bothering Remy.

I smile as I listen to their friendly bickering. Back to normal. And Remy's probably still so relieved that Dejan is free of the stoneheart, he's not going to kick him out.

My tac vest goes by my pack that's still shoved up against the wall. Longsword and dirk belt next. I toss my overshirt down and shrug out of the chain mail, draping it across the pack. I don't really feel like putting the fatigues shirt back on, so it gets folded up before I tug the sleeves of the remaining thermal up to my elbows.

When I turn around, Maya is hovering by the couch, fixedly avoiding looking at either of us. She clutches the water glass, the contents shivering a little.

"Need anything?" Cieran's question has her attention flying up to him. He straightens the hoodie he's pulled on and shoves hands in the pocket.

"I'm okay," she responds, then quickly looks away at the way he arches an eyebrow at her clenched and shaking hands.

"Why don't you sit down for a few minutes," Cieran says kindly.

Maya reflexively nods and edges around the corner of the couch and perches on the edge of the cushion. Cieran shoots me a look and I scowl back, just on principle. Any wordless retort he's going to make is cut off by the buzz of his phone.

Some of the lines ease up across his face as he answers. "Hey, hot stuff." Athina.

I find Maya looking back when I focus on her again. She quickly looks away. I fidget slightly. I'm rarely this unsettled at the thought of a conversation, and never with her. *Get it together.*

"Can I sit?" I ask, flicking a hand at the armchair angled to her position on the couch.

She nods silently, taking an almost desperate drink of water. I can't think of anything to say that's not just asking if she's okay for the hundredth time.

Cieran drops into the other armchair directly across the coffee table from me. "No," he says. "We're still going in circles." He leans on his knees, rubbing at his eyes with free hand. "Tell me you have agencies back on Kirnae that only irritate and interfere."

He chuckles. I half-smile. From the way his laugh deepens for a second, that's a resounding yes.

"Remy finally asked Alder out," Cieran tells her, half-laughing again. "Yeah."

Maya looks to me, smile toying at the corners of her mouth. "He did?"

I nod, not telling her that it was partially to make a point to me. But she grins at her water. They've heard about Alder, and Nadi was practically gleeful to report that Alder has been into the *Fox* more than once. It seems she's completely moved on from her longtime crush on Remy and is now actively engaged in Remy and Sara's "will they, won't they."

"I...um..." Maya glances to me, then quickly away. "I probably can't turn my phone on, can I?"

"No." I wince as I say it. "Did you need to call someone?" I'm almost scared to ask and see if she's actually got someone else and we are just really friends.

She wedges her hands cupped around the glass between her knees. "I just wanted to let Nadi know that I was okay. I did just abruptly leave the *Fox* without telling her, after we agreed on working a buddy system so I wouldn't be alone."

I soften. That does sound like Nadi. And she's probably tried to call Maya forty-five times. Though I haven't gotten a panicked message yet. I'm sure that Nadi knows at least something of what's going on.

I pull out my phone and proffer it. "If you want."

She smiles—a shadow of her normal expression—and sets her glass on the table before reaching for it. "Do I ask if she's under her name or something else in your phone?" Maya hesitates over the messaging icon.

"Just 'Nadi,'" I reply. "I don't follow her crazed method of naming everyone by some nickname."

Maya's grin turns to something slightly guilty, and I chuckle. "Please don't tell me you do the same."

She starts typing. "Maybe."

I lean on my knees, hands scrubbing at each other. "Dare I ask what I am?"

She glances at me, amusement bright in her eyes, sparking through the grey ringing her iris. "Commander Ryder."

My jaw drops momentarily. "Am I some sort of joke to you?" I protest.

She starts laughing, face scrunching as the sound borders on something closer to hysterical for a brief moment. "He's really cool!" she protests, unable to keep typing as humor still thrums.

"He *dies* in season two!"

"*Heroically!*"

I give her a doubtful look that only makes her laugh again. For a moment, we're back to how it was a few weeks ago, the unspoken weight gone between us.

"I'll allow it, only because it sounds like I'm cool and heroic," I say. She purses her lips and gives me a look that only makes me laugh and spread my hands in avoidance. "I didn't say it."

Laughter remains on her face as she finishes typing and sends the message. The phone hums almost immediately and she draws back midway through handing it back.

She starts typing again, pausing as mortification spreads over her face. "I am deleting these messages."

I chuckle. Nadi's not stupid and she's been gently teasing me about Maya for months. I've no comeback for her now. Maya and I are somewhere past "friends," but I might keep dragging my feet about asking where we actually are.

"Thanks." Maya hands me the phone, still shaking her head.

I slide the phone around and around between my hands as she retrieves her water. It seems like we're both afraid to say anything and ruin the easiness that's returned for a moment. I glance to Cieran. He leans on his knees, his thumb rubbing across his forehead.

"You still coming?" he asks Athina almost cautiously. "Yeah," he huffs. "We'll talk, I promise." Another pause. "I know. I love you." Cieran hangs up. He scrubs a hand through his hair and sighs quietly before standing and heading toward the kitchen.

"Are *they* okay?" Maya inclines her head toward where Cieran had been sitting.

I smile faintly. "Yeah, just in the middle of figuring out the 'what's next.'"

It looks like Cir still doesn't know, or is still avoiding the issue. But he and Athina are talking about it and are still able to have conversations around it. It always seemed like when Pothos and his wife argued, it was silence on both their ends. I told him to just talk to her way too many times.

"I'm assuming that 'deal with a drug lord and rescue the half-fae who stupidly called you' weren't part of their plan?" She's back to spinning the glass in her hands.

"Maya." I try to keep my voice light, but it seems to want to linger over her name every time I say it. She looks at me, and my heart starts racing at the emotion tangled up in her eyes. "This is not your fault."

"I know." Her voice hushes. "It's just...just that I..." She abruptly places the glass back on the table and squeezes her clasped hands between her knees. I hover on the edge of a breath, not sure what I'm going to say.

"Just that I feel like I'm ruining a lot of things by being here and being involved." She rushes over the words. And it seems like she forces herself to look at me. I reach out to her before I can stop myself. I'm about to pull back when she frees one hand and grabs mine. Honestly, it's not really helping the confusion, but my steady hand clasps gently around her shaking one.

"You're not," I tell her.

She inhales shortly, almost ruefully looking at our clasped hands. "Are you sure?" she whispers.

I swallow hard and take the plunge. "Sure like you think we'll be mad, or sure like you want me to let go?"

A faint smile crooks her mouth. "Do you want to let go?" It comes out low, like she's just as confused with where we stand.

"Not really," I tell her. A bit of hope bursts with her widening smile and the way she settles her hand more securely in mine.

"I don't really want you to," she says. A wider grin hits her face. "Unless you screw up our mission again and we don't get to Artemis Forge."

I roll my eyes as I chuckle. "That move has worked before."

She makes a disbelieving sound.

"*If* you two are done holding hands..." Remy interrupts with a smirk. He's holding two steaming bowls with chunks of bread balancing precariously along the edge.

Gleeful *ooohs* come from the peanut gallery and I shoot them a vaguely murderous look over Maya's head as she ducks in quick embarrassment.

"There's a no kissing rule in my apartment," Dejan calls.

Maya twists on the couch and shoots him what must be an epic glare based on his mock surrender along with an "I thought we'd bonded finally."

We all glance at him, a little surprised at this turn of events.

"Bet that rule changes once Tara gets here," Cieran remarks.

Dejan says something in elvish that has Cieran chuckling and pushing him out of the way to serve himself some food.

Maya turns back and takes the bowl from Remy. "Thanks." A smirk flashes on her face. "When's your date with Sara?"

I just laugh as I take the bowl from him along with a grieved look of betrayal. It doesn't last long before he easily tells her, "Tentatively next Friday."

Her frown says she understands that this means only if the mission is done. "Well." She clears her throat. "I'd offer to help fight bad guys except I don't have great control of my magic, and it sounds like I'm going to be holed up with chocolate and hopefully some way to watch *Starfall* over and over."

Remy chuckles. "You did a pretty good job earlier. I felt the residual of that blast you threw to get away. Nice job."

Some unexpected relief slides in at the sight of Remy easily talking to Maya about her fae magic, and the way he stands relaxed in short sleeves and not angling to try to hide his warlock tattoos.

I'm pretty sure she's flushing as she tells him "Thanks."

She pauses as I quietly bless my food and cross myself before digging in. Remy's brought it down to eating temperature.

"One of these days you might have to teach me a few prayers," she says, tearing off a bit of bread and dipping it into the soup. "I'm assuming there might be a patron saint of people with brothers in a gang."

I chuckle, relieved again at the way the stress seems to be leaving her, and her smiles have come back. "There probably is."

I'm trying not to read too much into her words. My faith is a huge part of who I am, and sharing it with someone has always been my hope. She offers a smile, but doesn't say more, applying herself fully to eating.

She's not bothered by the others coming in, or Dejan taking the other end of the couch as Cieran reclaims the armchair. Remy makes himself comfortable on the floor by the fireplace, stretching his legs out.

"This is really good," Maya says.

"Thanks," Remy replies.

"Do you have a recipe?" she asks.

He taps his head with a bit of apology.

"What kind of tea do I bribe you with to write it all down?" She leans forward.

He looks almost surprised, like the barista wouldn't notice he only ever gets tea when we go to the *Fox.*

"Just nothing floral." He grimaces.

"What do you have against sweet stuff?" Maya shakes her head. "No chocolate, no sweetened teas...?"

Remy shrugs easily. "Got to be bitter like me."

We chuckle and Maya rolls her eyes. Even she knows he's probably one of the most easy-going people you'll meet.

"Is that to be able to put up with Dejan?" she asks.

The elf snorts. "Yeah, she can stay." He smirks at me. I shake my head and Maya purses her lips.

Cieran sits by, a half-smile on his face as he eats. He talks about his old crew occasionally, and I wonder if this feels like echoes of what he had with them too. Families, significant others slotting in among dinners, getting along easily with each other and the crew. I know I wouldn't want it any other way.

He's distracted momentarily by his phone. He checks it, and then looks to Maya and me.

"Myerson's got a place for you tonight. After you eat, Besim can walk you over."

"Thanks," she tells him, and sends a quick smile at me. I return it, even though I don't want this time to end. Don't want to take her somewhere I can't protect her if she needs it. Even if my mind is trying to tell me that she's safest on base or in witness protection with the FBI, I don't want to let her go.

18

BESIM

DINNER FINISHES AND MAYA goes to grab her chocolate bar from the refrigerator. I pull on my overshirt and make sure a knife is in place. Like anyone will attack on base. But I'm also keyed into the more alert space that comes with missions. I have the address from Cieran and we both ignore the teasing as we leave the apartment.

"My experience is obviously limited, but I'm assuming they're always like that?" Maya asks as we get down to the sidewalk and I point us in the right direction.

I chuckle. "Yeah. Although, I'm due a little roasting with how much crap we've given Remy the last few months."

She tilts a look up at me. "Yeah, there's probably some sort of karma there."

We walk a little farther in silence as the dusk settles and the chill starts to deepen. Sunset is still throwing a few stray beams up above the horizon line and when Maya stops suddenly, I'm assuming it's to watch.

"I was going to run," she blurts out.

I swing to face her, still halfway processing what she said when she goes on. "After I left the *Fox*. I went home to pack and I was going to leave, but then Emmet showed up and..."

"Leave?" I say almost dumbly.

She shifts foot to foot, arms at her sides then crossing, over and over. "I just...I guess I don't know what I was thinking, really." A poor laugh trails the words.

I'm still stuck, her fluctuating responses making some more sense. "Would you have said anything?" I wince internally. What I should have said was "I'm glad you didn't," but she only didn't because she got kidnapped. And now I sound like I'm ten.

She focuses on her green sneakers, arms staying across her stomach. "I don't know. Maybe not until I'd settled somewhere."

Even though she didn't, even though she's standing right here, even though we just told each other that we'd like to be something more, something like betrayal rears up for a second before I can firmly quash it.

"I'm sorry," she whispers. "I..." Her shoulders lift in a sigh before she turns her brilliant eyes back up at me. "I haven't really...cared about someone other than my brother for years because he broke my heart a little. Haven't really let myself have friends for...for years. Have really just been scared to start trying to live for myself...And when I moved here, I told myself I was going to. And between the coffee shop and Nadi being the best friend I could ask for, and...and *you*."

The same breathlessness hits me watching her.

"I think part of it was I couldn't bear knowing you were going to run right into danger and maybe get hurt. Couldn't bear thinking that maybe some small part of this might be my fault. And what if I bring more or different trouble later if this isn't resolved, or..."

"Hey," I break in gently, reaching out between us. "That's a lot of what-ifs."

She smiles softly and takes my hand. It's my left, the one with burn scarring reaching up my entire arm, up my neck, and scattered across my lower jaw. She tentatively brushes against the scar with her thumb before tucking away like she's nervous of my response.

I still have a hard time sometimes with memories from the moments when I got hit with untamed wildfire magic in the Wastelands and it ate *through* my stoneskin to scar. Even almost a year later, when I've mostly been able to work through the worst, I'll sometimes still try to hide it. Her touch sends something electric up my arm, piercing into my heart.

"Part of me is still scared of what you do, of what might happen," she admits in a whisper. "I don't know what I'd do if you got hurt. I don't think I could bear it if…"

"Hey," I interrupt again, still just as gentle. "I'd lose my mind if something happened to you, okay. Ask them." I tilt my head in the direction of the apartments. "When Cieran came in and said you'd been taken, I couldn't get out of there fast enough."

A faint smile spreads across her face and her grip tightens in mine.

"I can't really tell you not to worry about me, but…but this is what I do. This is my job, and…" I'm not really sure what I'm trying to say. Maybe afraid that being a soldier is the deal breaker for her. But being in the service is the other part that makes me *me*. I know it's not for everyone to wait for soldiers to come back, but…

"I'd wait!" she blurts. "Fates, I'd wait for you to come back, Besim."

There's only enough air in my lungs for me to say, "You would?"

"Yeah." She half-laughs. "Yeah, I would. I will."

"Okay," I stammer. It's like I'm about to deploy for months on end, sent out to fight some never-ending war instead of being here in Dunhare and not leaving anytime soon.

She swipes at her eyes with her free hand. "I don't know why I'm crying. You're not going anywhere." She laughs again. "Right?"

"Not after that." I start to smile, and she laughs again.

"I don't know why I'm laughing either, I just...I think I've just wanted to tell you that for a while," she says. "Guess I wasn't sure you'd want *me*."

The slightly self-deprecating tone has me shaking my head.

"Why? Because you're smart, and funny, and you love a ton of the same stuff I do. You can put up with Nadi. And..." I stumble to a halt, distracted by the smile and the hope in her eyes. "And you're really beautiful. I figured you could do a lot better than me."

Her lips flatten, drawing my gaze there. "Really? I could do better than someone who's loyal and smart and honest and open and loves a ton of the same stuff I do? Who has an amazing family, and who I find to be really handsome?"

It brings heat and something like shyness that she thinks all those things of me. Part of me wants to deflect. Apparently I'm not great with compliments. But any thought of making my own self-deprecating joke is lost in the commotion that's her placing her free hand on my chest and stepping a little closer.

"And...and maybe I'd like to be someone you could lean on a little if you need."

My arm is around her before I know it, pulling her even closer. "I think I'd really like that."

My head tips down to her and she pushes up on her toes to meet me, lips pressing firmly against mine. I let go of her hand and slide mine around the back of her head, thumb brushing the edge of her jaw. Her lips part and I press a little. Her arms are around my neck, holding close until a small space exists to breathe.

A faint laugh escapes her. "I didn't think our first kiss would be right in the middle of the Army base on the way to meet a protective detail."

"So you thought about it?" I tease.

She shakes her head, laughter still sparkling in her eyes.

"I might be about to do it again," I say.

"I think I'd really like that," she replies. So I do.

A car driving by and honking breaks us apart. She presses her forehead against my chest, both of us laughing.

"I do need to finish taking you to meet the protective detail," I say regretfully. The sun has taken itself away and the streetlights are starting to fizzle on. Maya claims my hand as we turn back up the street.

"You won't be able to stay a few minutes, will you?" she asks.

I shake my head regretfully. "I've already probably been gone too long. You know how much crap they're going to give me when I get back?"

Maya leans into my arm as she chuckles. It's only a few more minutes' walk to the designated address. It's a family unit for one of the Guard members who lives on base with his wife and kids. Sergeant Aaron Rosser is a good guy, though with the way he's waiting on the darkened porch, arms crossed over his burly chest, it feels for a second like I'm walking Maya back home and am about to get a lecture from her dad.

"Antilles." Rosser nods. He's got a rumbling Louisianian accent. His shirt sleeves are pulled up to his elbows, showing some pale scars through his black skin.

"Sergeant," I reply and make the introductions. I don't miss the way Rosser arches an eyebrow at our hands still clasped. Rosser's wife pokes her head through the door. She flips the light, shaking her head at her husband who hadn't done it yet, perhaps preferring to stand in the near darkness. Two younger kids peer around the front window curtains before sidling off.

"Maya?" she asks, and extends her hand when Maya affirms. "We've got it from here, Specialist."

She's got the same easy accent, but a much freer smile than her husband. A bright red bandana ties back her natural curls.

Maya takes the first low step and turns to face me, closer to eye-level. "Thanks."

"We'll try to be around when the agents come pick you up tomorrow," I say, not ready to let her go.

Her fingers tighten in mine. "Goodnight."

"See you soon," I promise and open my hand. Regret fills her face and she backs up another stair.

"Seb going to be around?" Rosser's wife asks him. He nods back. "I'll get some lemonade made."

"Thanks," a low voice answers and bright orange light flares in her hand in response.

"Seb! What *have* I told you?" She flicks her hand at the far corner of the porch where I can now see a figure reclining in a wicker chair. His smile flashes in the harmless red sparks coming his way and doesn't move.

"Sorry, ma'am," The red-haired half-fae replies. He glances at me, showing the vibrant purple ring around his irises.

"I also told you to stop with that," she mutters ferociously. Seb and Rosser just chuckle and return to their silence. Maya pivots once and flashes me a "what are you leaving me with?" look. I just wave. She'll be fine. If anyone finds her or tries to attack, they won't see Rosser and Seb coming until it's too late.

"Thanks," I tell them. They just nod. You think Dejan doesn't talk much? Crew Three is even quieter. I leave, letting the sounds of voices and laughter from inside the house reassure me that Maya's going to be fine even though every part of me wants to stay.

19

Dejan

In the privacy of my room, I cue healing magic into my hand. Especially after today, I can't leave the others to face Damir alone. I need to be able to get back into the field. And that means being stupid for a second. A quick check through the heartbond returns quiet. Tara's asleep and that slightly lessens the guilt as I put up an extra mental wall to block what I'm about to do. It's something I was too good at years ago, but I don't want to wake her up in a panic if this sneaks through.

My face, I don't really care about. It's the still healing ribs and leg that need the attention. I press my hand against my ribs first, wincing as my magic readily leaps to the spiderweb cracks in the bones and knits them together, pulling another few weeks of healing into a few seconds. A grunt escapes as I pull my hand away and lean on my knees, combating lightheadedness. Tara doesn't stir. The dampener plus my extra mental block keeps this to myself. I grab the chocolate bar from the bedside table and eat a piece, letting it work for a second with its added fae-based regeneration spell laced in.

When the room stops tilting, I do the same for my leg. Pain recedes like a violent riptide leaving sweat trickling down my temple. I cram another few bites of chocolate. Hopefully Remy doesn't sense the amount of magic I just did and kick down the door. But all's quiet on the other side. They've settled.

I ease up on the heartbond block. Tara still doesn't flinch. I collapse the rest of the way into bed, barely able to pull the blankets up over my head. They shouldn't have left me unsupervised. Cieran can chew me out and I'll deal with the resigned judgment from Besim. But they're not leaving without me tomorrow.

———

I wake feeling closer to normal than I have in the last week, and definitely in three months since the stoneheart isn't blocking everything. And it takes two seconds for my phone to buzz.

"Dejan." Tara's voice filled with warning greets me as I answer.

"Good morning," I return. She just huffs and I feel a little prod through the dampened heartbond. It makes me smile.

"I don't know whether or not to yell at you for being stupid, or ask if you're doing all right," she admits.

"If it makes you feel better, I'm probably about to get yelled at for being stupid as soon as I walk out of my room," I say. She chuckles and I don't tell her that just hearing her voice is settling me further. And not making me regret last night in the slightest.

"Can't believe I feel like I've missed how exasperating you can be," she says, a light laugh coating her words.

"That's just my natural charm."

"Your natural BS," she retorts and I chuckle, settling my hand over my ribs to ease a little more magic into them and reduce the slight ache.

"*Are* you okay?" Tara's question is a little subdued, and I push reassurance back through the bond along with my words.

"Yeah, promise. You?" I ask after a moment.

She sighs. "Just wishing I knew when I could see you in person again."

I almost want to apologize for everything again, and for the life of unexpected deployments and no-contact missions she suddenly signed up for with the reactivated heartbond.

"Trust me," I say. "We're working as fast as we can." I glance at the clock. Speaking of which... "But I do need to go."

"Okay." It's filled with the same reluctance grabbing me. "Be careful. And"—Tara's voice shifts—"I do have everyone else's numbers so I *will* be contacting them if you do something stupid again."

I roll my eyes. Of course she has their contacts. But I'm not mad at all, instead sitting here in something like awe at the easy acceptance of her from my team and the way I'm absolutely unafraid to have her fully in my life.

"Love you, Tare," I say, and smile at the way she almost happily hums like the first time I ever told her that.

"Love you too," she replies. "And please be careful."

"I will," I say, and really do mean it. As I hang up, I half-smile again at the feeling of her happiness on the other side of the bond. I tug at the bracelet for a second, wishing I could take it off. But the only way to safely keep it off for awhile is to make sure this mission is done. And unfortunately, Damir isn't going to just leave without a fight.

When I dress and make it out to the main living area, Cieran watches me with narrowed eyes.

"You're looking suspiciously spry."

"Just got a good night's sleep." I shrug.

His raised eyebrow calls my bullshit louder than him actually saying it. "You have anything left in the tank?" he asks.

"I healed last night," I admit. "I actually did sleep really well. I'm good to go, Sarge."

He rolls his eyes at my actual use of the rank. Can I do any big healing on someone? Remains to be seen, but I can do a lot of my job without magic anyway. And now I can draw my bow without re-cracking my ribs. Yeah, I'm an idiot, but what else is new?

"I don't know how Pothos managed to keep up with all of you." Cieran shakes his head like he wouldn't have recklessly done the same. I tilt a smile, though part of me knows that Pothos wouldn't really have kept up. He wouldn't have said anything about me overdoing it, wouldn't have batted an eye. He's a good guy, a good soldier in many ways, but Cieran definitely keeps a closer eye on all of us than our old sergeant. We all know it, and are all grateful for it.

I head for the kitchen and some coffee, finding Remy at the table on video call with his family. A pile of bacon and toast already waits on the counter.

"No, Bear, I can't come home today," Remy says. He frowns at me as I pass by, noticing the same thing that Cieran did.

"I don't know when." Some tight frustration lines Remy's voice, especially as his son starts to almost scream, "I want you to come home!"

Remy's mom tries to get Blair to calm down and Remy rubs his forehead. "I know, Bear. I know. I want to come home too, but I can't yet, okay."

"Dad," Blair tearfully says. "I keep having badmares. You have to come back. You promised."

I wince. Bear's still having nightmares about being kidnapped three months ago. He's gonna break Remy's heart if he keeps this up.

"I know, Bear. Soon, okay?" Remy manages a smile, but the pain is evident everywhere around it. "Love you."

"Love you, Dad." Bear sounds almost like he's promising vengeance instead. Remy hangs up, and shoves the phone face-down on the table before resting his head on his arms. The wooden surface receives his plentiful curses.

I reach over and tap his shoulder. I've got no real support to offer other than that. I don't really know what it's like to leave someone behind every time we head out on mission.

"I knew I shouldn't have called," he mumbles.

"He's gonna be okay," I say.

"I know." A sigh rocks his shoulders, then he lifts his head. "What did you do?"

I try for innocent but it's so rare an expression that he sees right through it.

"What? Think I'm going to let you all go without me today?" I ask.

He huffs. "Bes said you were being stupid yesterday too."

I toss my hands wide. "Nothing's sacred with him."

Remy snorts a laugh. "It was pretty obvious. Just eat breakfast. I think we're headed out soon."

"Take it to go," Cieran says in sudden urgency. We both lean toward him where he scans his phone. "There was a hit on a building just a few minutes ago. Matches hits done by Shrikes. Napier's meeting us there."

Breakfast is forgotten in the rush to finish dressing and arm up. I get my armored tac vest on, the weight still pulling a little at my ribs, feeling only like I've got something small stuck in my shirt and poking my side. I can deal with that.

I string the bow just to check and am able to perform the action. But notice how over a week of recovery has lessened my normal strength. I unstring it and clamp it into the quiver holster.

We all take something to eat on the way. Eckhart meets us at the street with an Army issued truck. Remy takes the driver's seat, and Bes and I cram into the back.

I'm trying not to show that I'm breathing a little harder than normal as I settle. Besim politely doesn't comment, though I can feel the judgment.

It's a fifteen-minute ride, even with Remy's driving. We pull up at a building just outside the warehouse district. My stomach falls as I step out and see the ruined mess of the building. The second floor looks bombed out, brick and rebar fallen to the sidewalk below. Scorch marks spread across the ragged wound. Whatever exploded came from *inside*.

Teams of firefighters still work, using hoses and keeping their water warlocks in reserve if needed. Napier stands in his impeccable suit right at the established boundary. Evacuated inhabitants stand outside the tape barriers, clustered and gawking. A few news teams with cameras and reporters stand behind it as well, some trying to get Napier's or the fire chief's attention.

Two firemen come out of the building entrance, shaking their heads.

"Fire's out upstairs. Aren't going to need medics," one reports grimly.

Cieran ignores the nearest reporter as he goes to talk to the fire captain, letting him know that this might be ours and the FBI's case. Remy crouches next to a pile of smoking bricks, waving off a cautionary call from a firefighter. He brushes a hand across the brick, frowning at whatever he's pulled off it. Crew Five arrives and starts setting a perimeter, pushing the onlookers farther back.

Besim has eyes out like I should. But I'm staring at that gaping hole, the same writhing horror in my gut as seeing something like this for the first time in Detroit. My dad had brought me to see the results. I'd looked from the window of the car, halfway listening to him expound the value of loyalty and the punishment for betrayal that was our due to mete out as Kostics. I think that was the day I truly started to want *out*.

"See anything familiar?" Napier stands next to me, staring up at the destruction.

"You know I do," I reply through clenched teeth. "You going to blame me?"

"I'd really rather blame your cousin," the fae replies.

I offer a mirthless smile. "Why this building?" I ask.

Napier waits until Cieran comes over. "This is where we had our surveillance team headquarters."

Both of us visibly start and Remy swivels where he's still crouched.

"How'd they find it?" Cieran asks.

"I have some suspicions that I'd rather not voice out in the open," Napier says.

Cieran glances around, noticing what I'm finally picking up. "Where's your buddy?" he asks.

Napier smiles thinly. "Hopefully proving me wrong." He heads for the door. "Care to come along?"

"Cir." I jolt forward a step as Cieran makes to follow. "It's going to be..." I swallow hard. Whatever's up there, it's not going to be pretty.

Cieran's face slants in grim lines. "I know. You can stay down here if you want to." *If you don't want to see your cousin's work again.* He knows I'm not squeamish.

I slide thumbs around my vest straps. "Let's go."

"Rem." Cieran jerks his head at the door. I don't want either of them to see what Kostics can really do. Don't want them to see *this*, even if we've seen it and worse before.

Remy taps my shoulder and follows Cieran inside. I'm a half-step behind.

The stench of burning hits immediately, and dust trickles from the ceiling. This building looks old and run-down like the others next to it. Cheap housing due to the proximity to the shadier dock areas nearby. The explosion probably didn't do its survival instinct any favors.

Stairs creak warningly under our weight. Remy's hands swing by his sides, ready to call up magic if needed. Cieran steps light, and Napier shows caution for the first time in our brief acquaintance.

He stops at the top of the stairs and Cir waves Remy forward first. Soot and residual magic cake the hallway. The magic stirs dust in lazy eddies, a few shimmering lines visible in a blast pattern. The invisible magic brushes against us like static. Debris piles, and the walls cave outward into the hallway. Fluorescent lights dangle from wires, shredded bits of drywall and insulation waver in a faint draft coming from the torn exterior.

Remy carefully sets one foot on the top of the stairs and deep blue flickers around his hand. He inhales and his stance widens slightly. Centering himself to make sure his magic is firmly set to his core, reducing the danger of overdrawing in emergency.

He lifts his right hand, bringing it even with his heart, then stepping quickly up into the hallway. His left hand sweeps around before gently tapping his chest.

A sigh thrums through the hallways, and the prickle against my skin lessens. Napier tilts his head, shoulders twitching like he's relieved to get rid of the lingering magic.

Remy walks forward slowly, tapping his boot with each strike, testing the ground stability while he clears. We wait, patient. We're not about to casually walk forward before Remy finishes clearing.

You can always trust Besim's advice and you can always trust Remy's magic. Those might as well be part of the Drax creed. Or part of Besim's commandments.

Remy gets to the end of the hall and moves his hands in a weaving pattern before tapping his chest again, this time with his right hand. Everything sags more, and even Cieran feels the magic leaving by the way he shifts on his feet.

"All clear, Sarge," Remy calls.

Cieran taps Napier's shoulder, keeping the agent back and letting someone else test the hallways first. I'd have let the fae take his chances, but Cieran's better than me, especially right now.

I gesture for Napier to follow when Cieran makes it safely. The fae gives a thin smile and joins the others as I stay at his six.

And it's bad.

We all stare into what's left of the FBI surveillance headquarters. Something was detonated in the middle of the room. My guess, it was thrown inside by the way some of the twisted remains look like they might have been trying to dive away.

Charred husks might have been computers or cameras at some point. Doesn't look like anything is left for Besim to work his own particular magic. I'm betting that any intel the team gathered is destroyed.

"You have any backups?" Cieran asks.

Napier seems to only have a staid expression or that narrow smile that doesn't hold any matching emotion. "They hadn't sent someone to deliver the newest batch of drives."

"So there's backup somewhere?" Cieran presses.

"Cason has it all."

A prickle hits my arms at the way he says it, like we might have to run a mission to recover it. Cieran glances his way, eyes narrowed slightly.

"We'll send someone up to gather the bodies," Cieran says. There's not much point in us investigating the origin or those responsible. I can confirm who did it. "How'd Damir find this place? I thought it was secure."

Now we're getting to it. Napier pulled us off our own surveillance yesterday since this was his solution. The fae glances around like the bodies are going to tell secrets.

"There's a leak somewhere. Potentially very close to me," he says.

Cieran studies him closely. "Cason?"

"I hope not. I'm running my own investigation alongside this, Sergeant. I can't trust anyone." He flicks a glance at me. I'm not the only one scoffing at the implication, but he doesn't retract it. "This is part of the reason I wanted your team to pull back. I didn't want to risk more than one team."

"So you'd sacrifice your own people?" Cieran asks, a bit of anger stirring around him.

I'm really starting to hate Napier's smile. "They knew the risks. They were supposed to start pulling out."

Cieran shakes his head and turns back toward the stairs. "Let's go."

"I know you've made difficult calls, Sergeant," Napier says.

Cieran stalks back. Remy throws a disgusted glance out of the corner of his eye as he puts distance between the fae and himself. Our sergeant halts a bare pace from the agent. He's not concerned at all about any magic the guy might throw. Remy spreads his fingers wide, ready for anything. I'm planning to hang back and watch Napier get pummeled.

"There's a difference between difficult calls and leaving your men to get killed on a hunch," Cieran spits out. Napier doesn't flinch, and doesn't offer any move or word to defend himself or rebuff.

Cieran pivots again and leaves without being stopped this time. We follow, leaving Napier behind. Cir's cursing in a few different languages as we get to the bottom and step back into the cleaner air. He gives the all-clear for the cops to go in with body bags.

"Bad?" Besim asks.

Remy replies as I rub at my side, some odd new sensation pressing against the area. Caution tape flutters in a sharper wind. I avoid looking at the building, absently rubbing my chest as Besim comes to stand beside me.

He doesn't ask, just waits. And since I've got something bothering me, I talk. "I don't know what else to do."

He angles a look at me. "To?"

"Separate myself from the Kostic legacy." I jerk my chin at the building. "Feels like it's always one step beside me."

"You always take responsibility for everyone else's actions?" he asks calmly.

"I could have been part of this," I say, somehow angry even though I'd sacrificed almost everything to get out.

"Could have," Besim says slowly. "You aren't."

I shake my head, opening my mouth, but he beats me to it. "Yeah, I know. I'm right again." A smirk creases his features and I gently shove his shoulder. He claps my back. "Stop holding on to *what-if's* that would have never happened."

"Seriously, do you have these all written down in a book somewhere?" I ask.

"I just have frequent opportunity for practice," he says.

The pressure in my chest grows. I must be overdoing it somehow. I loosen a strap on my vest, hoping that'll help. But the feeling of *wrong* intensifies.

"Dej?" Besim asks when I don't give some sarcastic rejoinder.

Pressure builds and I stumble backward into the wall, heart racing and something foreign roiling inside me.

"Something's wrong." I pull at my vest but it refuses to budge. "Something's *wrong*!" Blood roars in my ears.

Remy appears in front of me, his hands frantically pushing mine aside, searching. "Where?"

"*Something's wrong!*" is my only reply.

"*Where?*"

Sudden clarity hits when the muted terror pummels my chest, racing alongside my heartbeat. The heartbond is trying to tell me. Warn me. But it's blocked by the dampener on my wrist.

"It's Tara," I whisper in horror.

Realization dawns over Remy's face. "Shit."

It hits me like a freight train. Something's wrong with *Tara*.

20

Dejan

I push against Remy, struggling to get away and...do what, I'm not sure. He pushes back, leveraging his slightly bulkier build against me.

"Dejan!"

"It's Tara!" I almost scream at him.

"Wait!" Remy keeps me pinned, making me only more frantic.

"Something's *wrong*!" I grab his shoulders, trying to get him to understand.

"Dejan." Cieran's sharper voice cuts in. I stop long enough to look at him, finding the understanding I want in his face. "Take a breath," he orders. "Rem." He taps the warlock's shoulder only after I obey. The pressure of Remy's hold loosens incrementally.

"What's going on?" Cieran asks.

"It was just sudden panic, and..." Fear. It'd been fear.

"Okay, could it have been something at the camp?" he asks, trying to help me parse through it. He's had the bond for almost a year and is way more in tune with his heartbond than Tara and I ever were. Though I'd kill to have the mental communication like him and Athina right now.

I shake my head. "Nothing patient related." Tare's got nerves of steel when it comes to anything medical.

"Okay, call her."

Remy fully releases me to let me grab my phone from one of the front pockets of my tac vest. I fumble to unlock it, forced to stop when an incoming call sets it to vibrating. I stare at the number. Not Tara's. The burner phone Maya is supposed to have. My own dread hits and I answer.

"You don't look so good, cousin." Damir's voice cuts me off before I can say anything.

"Damir," I hiss. Remy spins around, blue wicking around his wrists, ready to be thrown into a shield. Cieran waves to Besim and the other crew and everyone stills into alertness. The firefighters and cops pause, moving to shelter behind trucks, some waving the still lingering civilians farther away.

"Though you seem practically…vibrant…compared to the last time we saw each other," Damir continues. "I couldn't quite believe it when I heard you weren't dead."

Heard. Last thing he should have known about me was me lying unconscious on the ground, as good as dead if not for Tara.

"Who you talking to?" I grit out. The other side of the heartbond is still in turmoil and it's threatening to tear me apart.

"*I* don't normally spill family secrets," he *tsks*. "Is that a heartbond dampener?"

I jerk forward a step, trying desperately to figure out where he is. Damir's laugh grates across the connection.

"Now that is *interesting*." Motion across the street draws my attention. Damir lingers in the shadows between the row of abandoned apartment buildings. He wears his tailored suit pants and vest like armor. One hand holds the phone to his ear, the other spins a knife between his fingers like he can't wait to sink it into my heart.

A hand descends on my shoulder, holding me back from sprinting to meet him and present him with my own knife. I can see his smile.

"Literally always just holding you back, De'janick." He shakes his head. "Though it sounds like very soon I'll be able to see what happens in a heartbond. Don't bother calling the good doctor. I'll tell you where to find her. Though maybe not before it's too late." He steps back into the shadows and disappears.

Besim tightens his hold as I try to lunge toward the spot where Damir vanished.

"He's got her!" I'm fighting again, trying to tear away. "He has Tara!" I'm pleading with him to let me go. Cieran grabs the straps of my vest. I almost think he's going to shout at me, but he doesn't. Just holds tight. It's the agonized understanding in his eyes quickly fading to resolve that finally stills me.

Until Remy sprints by and throws up a shimmering blue shield as an explosion rocks the ground. Crew Five's magic user races to help shore it up as another detonation releases compressed wild magic to tear through the already shattered apartment buildings across the street. Screams from the civilians are dull echoes in my ears.

Cieran's got his shield out, and Besim's stoneskin glints silver in the flickering light of magic impacting against defensive shields.

The paramedics are already racing to check for injuries and I let them work, settling my hand on my sword.

"Set!" Remy shouts over his shoulder. He's about to drop his shield. Crew Five's air warlock shouts the same. Cieran and their sergeant bark orders and we fall into formation.

I'm caught between listening to Cieran, making sure Remy's not overdoing it, and still feeling that same roiling emotion from Tara. Or it's just mine under the sickening knowledge that Damir has Tara and he's going to make me suffer with anything he does to her.

Remy and the other warlock drop shields and we move forward with them in the lead, magic still swirling around their wrists. Rem's got his basalt blade out to help channel his magic into something even stronger. We make it through the now-ruined apartments, cross another street, then pause in the shelter of another set of crumbling buildings.

"The warehouse is just around the corner," Cieran murmurs through comms. "But I don't think he's stupid enough to just fall back there."

"Odds of getting another surprise like that?" the other sergeant asks grimly.

"High," is Cieran's reply. He taps Remy's shoulder where the warlock crouches in front of him. Remy just nods and the crisp scent of his magic appears along with a bit of heat that drives the lingering chill away.

"Go," Cieran orders and we push to motion again, coming around the corner as Crew Five emerges down the street in a pincer move heading straight for the warehouse.

We make it three steps before the warehouse implodes.

Remy's magic flares again, this time in a much smaller shield just around us as we drop to the ground in response. Through the shimmering blue, I can see Crew Five's warlock similarly protecting his team. It's seconds before the sound fades out and it's just the slight humming of Remy's magic. A few pieces of debris *clunk* off the barrier and then stillness settles.

A bead of sweat trickles down Remy's face as he drops the shield. I reach out to tap his shoulder and he gives me a thumbs-up in response, eyes still out and assessing for more threats. He just needs a break from casting and some chocolate. Not in danger yet of overdrawing his magic and getting into real trouble.

Distant sirens pick up and there's a clamor from behind where the first responders and civilians are no doubt panicking at the second explosion. We get to our feet, slowly sweeping forward toward the twisted ruins of the warehouse.

Remy crouches and presses fingers to the concrete. "No heat signatures. Nothing alive around here but us," he reports.

Crew Five's warlock cups his hand then flicks his fingers, a chill breeze cutting across the ruins. "Only residual magic is the implosion. Someone had to set that spell, but it's covered up any gate or circle they'd use to get out."

Meaning he or Remy can't backtrace a portal gate or transport circle to wherever Damir went. That's probably only half the reason he blew the warehouse. He probably meant to take some of us with it.

"Start setting a perimeter," Cieran tells Five. "I'll send the fire team over to make sure it's cleared." He waves to us and starts heading back to the bombed apartments.

It takes only a few seconds for the firefighters to leave and Napier to push in asking questions. Cieran ignores him and focuses on me. "Call Tara."

I obey. Right to voicemail. My hands start to shake again. Especially as I realize...I can't feel the heartbond. I grab at my tac vest again like I can reach into my chest and find the bond and Tara.

"Dej?" Remy is at my side again.

"I can't feel it," I whisper. He stills and a quick intake of breath and something that might almost be a curse comes from Besim. My knees shake and Remy's grip on my arm anchors me from falling into roiling panic.

Cieran pulls out his phone and hits call. "Hey, you still at the camp? I just need to know if Tara is still there." He looks to Napier. "She got picked up this morning by two agents."

I try again. Immediate voicemail.

Napier frowns and produces his own phone to start making calls. I'm locked in place, parsing back through the moments of heading to the warehouse, the explosions. I would have felt it if something happened to her, even with the heartbond dampener. If she...I refuse to even think that she's *gone.*

Cold washes over me, but it only heightens the panic thrumming through my limbs. Damir's not going to kill her yet. Not until he can make sure I feel every last moment.

"Is she alive?" Remy asks quietly.

I jerk a short nod. "They must have blocked the heartbond." And more anger rises at the thought of them using iron on her. Remy presses my shoulder, and I barely meet his look long enough to thump a fist against his chest.

Napier paces back and forth, arguing with someone. I don't care. I *need* to know where she is. Cieran's grip on my shoulder stops me from grabbing the agent's phone and demanding answers.

"I know," Cir says. He knows what he'd do, we all know what he'd do if it was Athina. And he'd be expecting us to help keep him in check and keep a level head long enough to get her back. I give a short nod of reassurance, and he slowly releases me.

Napier hangs up and looks to me. The first genuine emotion I've seen from him spreads over his face. Apology mixed with worry. "I just got off the phone with the agents who were supposed to bring Doctor Novak here tomorrow. They said they were ordered to stand down. By Agent Cason."

I'm about to stab something and it might be the fae. "Then who took her?"

"I don't know yet, but I'm willing to bet some of Damir's men stuffed into suits," the agent replies like I'm stupid. His eyes narrow and he starts making another call. "Has anyone picked up Miss Lyons yet?" he asks.

Besim jolts. I return the favor from earlier and jerk a hand in front of him like I could actually halt him.

Napier curses fluently in Gaelic. He shoves the phone away. "Cason picked up Maya forty minutes ago. They haven't made it to the safe house yet. Something tells me he's not taking her there."

21

Maya

I wave goodbye to Mrs. Rosser and her kids, grateful for the food and quiet night. Sergeant Rosser stands on the porch in the same spot as last night. If I hadn't seen him come inside and interact with his wife and kids like a totally different guy, I'd have believed he didn't leave the porch at all.

"Got everything?" he asks gruffly.

I lift my empty hands. "Everything I came with." Although I'm leaving in a clean T-shirt from his wife and a hair tie around my wrist to contain my curls later if I need to.

His mouth doesn't really smile, but his eyes do. I give a more open gesture. "Thanks for everything."

"Good luck." Rosser nods, falling back to the very intimidating soldier as a dark SUV pulls up and Agent Cason steps out from the driver's side.

I draw in a short breath and square up my shoulders. The agent halts at the bottom of the stairs and flashes a friendly grin.

"Ready to go?" he asks. I send one more glance down the street, hoping for some sign of Besim. Any of the crew would do really. I just don't want to feel like I'm going into this alone. I'm assuming since they're not here, something came up. And that makes the knots tighten.

"Yeah." I manage to head off my thoughts from spiraling into complete doom. One more wave to the Rossers and then I slide into the backseat. Cason shuts the door and circles around to the driver's side.

"Just you?" I ask, frowning at the empty car.

"Yeah, everyone's spread a bit thin with this case," he says. I watch some cop shows, but that doesn't mean they're accurate at all. I should probably trust the guy who actually does this for a living.

My phone's still an unusable brick in my back pocket. I've missed class, haven't been able to check email, haven't been able to text Besim nonstop...

"Is there a phone or computer I'd be able to use when we get there?" I ask.

He glances at me in the rearview. "Anything important?"

I grimace a little. "Classes."

"Ah." He nods. We fall to chatting about college and classes. What it takes to be an agent. How long he's been with the FBI.

And it's only when we pause that I realize I'm not really sure where we are. We've been driving for over fifteen minutes. I study the landscape flashing by and twist to look out the back. We're across the river. Which is a little weird.

"How much longer?" I ask, hands sliding between my knees.

"Not much." He gives another smile. But something's started to itch along my arms. I get that it's a safe house so he's not handing out addresses. But he really hasn't said much of anything specific.

I've just made up my mind to ask again when he makes another turn and pulls to a stop. It's the warehouses on the other side of the river. A few semitrucks are parked down the street. It's still early enough that there's not a ton of activity around. The main port is on the other side of the river. This is an odd place for a safe house.

The suited figure coming out of the nearest warehouse allays some suspicions. Until he opens my door and grabs my arm. I reflexively try to rip away, but stinging engulfs my wrist. Shock and horror freezes me along with the iron around my wrist. He reaches across, trying to grab my other wrist to close off the handcuffs.

I start fighting. Kicking, scratching. Even one iron cuff is enough to suppress my magic. I can still pull some, but not if he gets that last cuff set. I land a punch across his face, my sneaker connecting with his kneecap. He stumbles back enough for me to burst out of the car and start running.

I slam to a halt mid-stride. A whimper locks in my throat. I can't move, can't scream. But I can feel another mountain of betrayal as Emmet circles around me, regret and resignation in the shake of his head.

Hands grab me and Emmet drops the holding spell so they can wrench my wrists together and finish cuffing me, sealing off my magic. The iron burns against my skin. Thankfully I'm not full fae or I'd already have third-degree burns from the iron's suppressive counter. Iron won't kill fae or half-fae like it did in the Middle Centuries, but it can still *burn*.

I'm yanked forward, stumbling as I go. I'm too shocked and numb to really try to fight back this time.

The bright morning sunlight cuts out abruptly as we enter the building. It takes seconds for my eyes to adjust and when they do, my heart stalls yet again.

Damir Kostic stands in the center of the room, hands in pockets. "Welcome back, Miss Lyons. Let's try this all again, shall we?"

22

BESIM

"Bes," Cieran warns, hand extended toward my chest. He could stop me if he had to. Every bit of me is screaming to move, find Maya. Get Tara. I curl my hands into fists, trying desperately to recenter. All I can do is jerk a nod.

I don't have any way of knowing that Maya is still alive or unhurt. All I've got are prayers to guardian angels and the entire Trinity to keep her safe. The St. George medal on my tags digs into my chest as I shift restlessly. He's watched over me plenty. Hopefully he'll watch over Maya as we go fight some more dragons.

"Dej, see if you can pinpoint which way—"

But Dejan shakes his head, already cutting Cieran off. "They've blocked the heartbond. I can't feel anything for now." The elf stands still, but small tremors run through him. It's not going to be pretty when he's finally unleashed.

Cieran rubs his forehead, dislodging his hat for a moment before cramming it back on. "Rem, can you track Damir off some of Dejan's blood?"

Remy lifts a shoulder. "I can try. Direct siblings or blood will give an accurate target. Cousins would be like working with something more diluted. Might skew the results."

Dejan scowls. Cieran hooks hands in his vest collar. "We've got nothing on Maya either?" He looks to me. I shake my head.

A harsher expletive escapes him. I'm about to join Dejan in vibrating impatiently between praying for a miracle.

"Rem, see if you can—" Cieran cuts off with a frown and pulls out his phone. "Hello?" His brow furrows. "Marko?"

We all exchange a glance of similar confusion. I'd honestly thought we'd seen the last of the elf when he ran off with Cieran's number a few days ago.

"Hold up." He pulls the phone away and puts it on speaker. "Repeat that."

"I was just minding my business when I saw Bluejay's doctor get pulled out of a car by some Shrikes," the young elf says, voice low.

Dejan strides forward. "Where?"

"Are you guys always together?" Marko asks.

Dejan looks like he's about to reach through the phone and strangle the kid.

"Where are you, Marko?" Cieran breaks in.

"I'd found a place to stay by the docks," Marko says. "I'm not doing anything wrong by being here."

"I know," Cieran says patiently.

"It's by the river. I found an old pay phone to call you. It's just down the street from the place I saw."

I pull out my tablet, flipping to a program and entering Cieran's number. It loads and loads and then a map view appears. Red dot is Cieran, blue dot across the river is the pay phone originating the call.

"What else did you see?" Cieran asks.

"There's a lot of guys," Marko says doubtfully.

"Did anyone else get brought in?"

"Yeah, there was another lady who got brought by a suit a little bit ago."

My heart slams against my chest so hard I almost drop my tablet.

"What did she look like?" Cieran forestalls me. Dejan's hand on my arm surprises me.

"I think she's half-fae. Black. Real scrappy. Tried to get away." He sounds impressed.

"Tried?"

"Yeah, they got her in a spell and put cuffs on before they took her inside."

Dejan's hand slams into my chest. The same muted and helpless anger shines bright in his eyes.

"Okay. You have any idea how many people are around?" Cieran asks.

"There's like six guys just around front. They look loaded with magic. Sorry, Bluejay. Don't know if you guys can take them." He actually does sound genuinely nervous for us.

Cieran gives a mirthless smile, echoed by the rest of us. "Don't worry, Marko. We've had it worse. Listen to me, get out of there and get somewhere a lot safer, understand?"

"I can take care of myself, Jay," Marko snorts.

"I know. But all hell's about to break loose over there. You don't need to be around for that."

"Okay." Confusion laces Marko's voice, surprised maybe that someone cares.

"Thanks for calling. You helped us out a lot."

"Yeah." Marko's back to careless. "Hey, Bluejay...be careful." And the line slams shut.

A hint of a smile tugs Cieran's mouth as he puts the phone away. He looks at the map I've still got. "Okay, I'll route Crew Three that way to meet us."

"Let's go." Dejan practically spits it. He's visibly shaking now with anger and helpless rage.

"Dejan," Cieran warns. "What do you feel?"

The elf pauses for just a moment. "Still nothing."

"Don't take that off." Cieran points to the heartbond dampener. Dejan starts to argue but the sergeant cuts him off. "If Damir does anything, it'll keep you upright."

That shuts Dejan up. Nothing else from Tara. And we're all refusing to believe that's bad.

"Why's he calling you 'Bluejay'?" Napier asks.

"Slang for cop," Cieran replies.

"You're not cops," the agent says.

"That's what I keep telling him," Cieran calls over his shoulder as he leads the way to the truck.

23

Maya

"You're resourceful, I'll give you that," Damir says.

Fear takes up its residence again, freezing any words in my throat and threatening to keep accelerating my heart rate. Confusion is the only thing stopping me from passing out. Why am I here instead of in a safe house with FBI agents?

Agent Cason stands just off to the side, looking around with slight disdain. No one is shocked to see him here, and he's not pulling a weapon on Damir. The Butcher follows my look and scoffs a light laugh.

"Everyone's got a price, Miss Lyons," he says. "Do you have one?"

I clamp my lips shut. I don't know if I do, but I think I'd be on my knees begging if anyone I loved got hurt. For the first time in our—fortunately brief—acquaintance, some humor sparks in Damir's eyes.

"You the sacrificial type?" It's eerily like he can read my mind. "Is that why you get along with the make-believe heroes?" he asks, continuing when I don't answer. "What if I did something to your brother?"

Emmet's still at my side, and he doesn't even flinch at the threat. I look at him. He's impassive, like this is some sort of test. I'm not sure how to pass.

"We have different views on family," I say, my voice hoarse in parched throat.

The amusement fades. I said the wrong thing, even if it is true to me.

"You know he asked for you to stay safe in all this?" Damir gets close. I step back, slamming into something solid.

"He shouldn't have let you pull me in." I clamp my mouth shut but the words are out too fast, too angry.

Damir studies me, cataloguing every breath, every twitch, every bead of sweat forming at my temple. He's too close, the cuffs are burning, and I'm *trapped*.

"Most people are a whimpering mess by now," he says. A flash barely registers in my brain before cold steel presses to my cheek just under my right eye. If he's trying to get me to break down, he's getting really close. But something deep inside prods me to keep standing tall, keep looking back at him.

"Well." Damir withdraws, sliding the knife back into its sheath. "You've got potential, Maya."

I don't like that we're suddenly on first name basis.

"You're smart, scrappy. You're afraid, but you try to master it. Unlike many, many people." He sticks hands in his pockets, feet braced wide. It's a coiled posture, deceptive in its easiness. Dejan definitely wears the position more casually. "Morality only gets you so far. I could use someone like you around."

"No," I whisper, my voice wavering.

His lips curl at the corner. "Well, why don't you think about it. I've got an impending appointment with my cousin and his dogs." He glances over his shoulder.

My heart thuds faster again, though this time a beat closer to hope. Is the team on their way? Just as fast, the emotion vanishes, wiped out like flame in a void of air. *Am I the bait?*

"She didn't give any real information on who helped her," Cason says. His disdain is turned to me now.

Calculating lifts the corners of Damir's mouth again. "Hunnar," he calls.

Cold sweeps down my arms as the dark-haired elf comes over. A butterfly bandage spread-eagles across his temple and bruising spreads down his cheekbone. He doesn't look at me.

"Sir?"

"Cason here thinks that you're an undercover cop." Fake friendliness lightens Damir's voice, inviting us all to chuckle with the joke.

Hunnar tucks hands into his leather jacket. "That's something to say." He doesn't bother to hide his disgust of Cason.

"Klein recommended you highly. I'd hate to think that Maya here got away because of you." Damir's hands haven't moved from his pockets, but muscles in his forearms stand out in sudden sharpness.

"I've got a bruised shoulder and busted head that says she got away by throwing a blast of magic that cracked the sidewalk while she was at it. I was too busy being half-conscious on the sidewalk to do much," Hunnar replies. He doesn't seem concerned.

Cason's insistence on knowing if they were deep cover is making more sense. More secrets to sell. What if I accidentally threw Hunnar and his wolfhound shifter companion to the sharks? My heart ratchets up to a new speed. Damir glances to me, but I make sure my focus is on Hunnar as I pull back, like I'm afraid of him and what he'll do.

I've never been a great actor, but I'm praying to the general direction of everyone Nadi and Bes insist are in heaven to help me sell this. They must, since Damir chuckles.

"Fact remains that someone did help her after she unfortunately scuffed some of your reputation, Hunnar. Some shifter. Cason says that there's no FBI shifter around."

Hunnar shrugs. "Good Samaritan? Undercover cop? Maybe he's on that drive?"

Damir chuckles and frees a hand to pat over a vest pocket. "Klein is persistent. When I have my cousin's head, he'll get it."

Hunnar gives the same sort of smile that doesn't reach any higher than the corners of his mouth.

"Anything you want to do with Miss Lyons for that discomfort yesterday?" Damir asks.

I don't have to fake the retreat back into the man still holding me. Emmet's suddenly closer, but I don't want to think about him.

Hunnar flicks a glance to me and shrugs. "I don't need to rough up a woman to prove what a big man I am. She got the drop on me. I deserve a few bruises for that."

Damir's chuckle holds a bit of bewilderment to my ear. "A code like yours is rare these days."

Hunnar inclines his head. "If we don't have a code, then who are we, sir?" It seems like he throws a challenge with the words.

Damir huffs. "Klein doesn't know what he has." He shakes his head. "The job offer still stands."

Hunnar shrugs with a nod of acknowledgment. "Get your cousin's head, and I'll think on it."

Damir laughs, and it's an unexpectedly free sound. Whatever he says in reply is lost in the wave of his hand, and the man holding me shoving me to a walk. We head for the back corner of the warehouse where a blonde female elf sits, cuffed hands resting on drawn up knees. Dirt smudges her face and my eyes are about two seconds from joining her in being teary and red-rimmed. I get shoved down next to her, my knee scraping raw against the concrete.

The man tugs at the cuffs around my wrists, checking them. A breath catches in my chest as I look, *really* look, at him. The New Jersey warlock from the *Fox* looks grimly back, tips a slight wink that's not very reassuring before he walks away and leaves us alone.

But it's not like there's anywhere for us to go. Our spot is visible from almost any point, and there's so many men around that we wouldn't get very far even if we tried. Fear starts to really set it claws in and I start shaking uncontrollably as my back slams against the wall.

"Hey." The elf's cuffed hands settle on my arm. "You're okay, take a breath." Her voice is calm and kindly.

My attempt to obey is like pulling air over notches and grooves, hitching with each impact. Two more tries results in progressively smoother inhales.

"There," she says and removes her hold. I focus on her. Her hands hadn't been shaking at all when she'd touched me, but now a tremor runs through the iron loops connecting her cuffs.

"Are *you* okay?" I sniff.

"Can we put a pin in that question?" she replies, and a cheap imitation of a laugh comes from me. Her trembling smile answers.

"I'm Maya." I extend a cuffed hand.

"Tara." She shakes it. "First time being kidnapped?"

I already like her. Nothing like trauma to bond women. "Second actually. They tried yesterday."

"Last week was my first time." She tries to smile like she's delighted to discover we have so much common life experience.

"Third time, I'm voting to be taken to a spa."

She chuckles and some of the shaking in both of us reduces. I pull my knees up, and cram my hands into the small space of my lap. There's a hustle of activity like they're prepping for something.

Familiarity nags the back of my mind. I know her name. "Wait!" I sit a little taller. "You know Dejan?"

"Yeah." The way she smiles tells me everything. It fades into something miserable. "That's part of the reason *he* grabbed me." She rubs her nose. "Dej is going to do something so stupid, I know it."

A smile tugs my mouth. "Oh, they all might." I have no idea if they even know I didn't make it to the safe house. And after Besim's declaration yesterday, I'm not sure that I *want* him to know I'm in danger, because I don't want him doing anything idiotic either.

"You know the crew too?" Tara asks.

"Yeah, I work at Besim's sister's café." Nadi also doesn't need to know about two kidnappings in twenty-four hours because she's going to lose her mind.

"Wait, you're *Besim's* Maya."

I pull back a little. "How...?"

"Oh, Dejan texted me almost immediately." A faint grin brightens her features.

I narrow my eyes. "And he called Besim a snitch," I mutter. She chuckles.

Cold starts to seep through my jeans and chill my lower back. I've been kidnapped. Complaining about how uncomfortable the floor is should be the lowest priority. I shift again, going still when I realize.

I still have my phone.

Tara nudges my arm with her elbows. "What?" she furtively whispers.

"I have my phone." My lips barely move.

"They're going to notice you pulling that out," she hisses in warning.

"No." I look to her. "I just need you to turn it on."

"What?" She stares.

"Nerd stuff." I smile slightly before inching forward and angling just enough to put my right back pocket in her reach. She mutters something and slowly leans over.

"Sorry," she mumbles as she awkwardly sticks her cuffed hands around my phone. It takes three seconds for her to hold the power button and withdraw. My phone vibrates, alerting me that it's ready to go. But my breath has frozen again. Emmet is looking right at us.

I wait for him to raise the alarm, to come over and snatch the phone and any chance that Besim might even realize my phone's back on. If he hasn't already disconnected his access to the tracker. I really hope that sometime in the last few hours he didn't remember to be a gentleman.

My brother studies me, then slowly, deliberately, turns away.

24

Besim

The arrival of two more crews and a few cruisers full of police officers halt us from immediately leaving. I rub my forehead, trying to ignore the rising anger and frustration. A faint chime alerts me just before a red dot appears on the tablet map. I frown and tap it. My heart stops, then restarts at high speed.

Maya.

There's no reason for the Shrikes, or Cason, to know that I'd tagged her phone. Which means she must have found some way to turn it on.

"What?" Remy asks, craning his head to look at the screen.

"It's Maya," I reply. That blip is a miracle, a bit of hope. She's okay. She has to be okay.

"That our warehouse?" Cieran appears. He tugs the tablet from me when I make no immediate answer, halfway praying in relief and restarting the same prayers of protection for her and Tara. "Looks like it." He enlarges the view slightly and maneuvers it to check streets and start planning a route.

"We need eyes on before I figure out how we're going to hit this. Load up." He hands the tablet back. His full *sergeant* look sweeps between Dejan and me, warning us not to do anything stupid yet.

Dejan says nothing, just heads for the truck. Remy waits for me to follow before circling around and sliding into the driver's seat. Cieran's already on the radio, coordinating with the other team and with Crew Three on the way.

My hands clasp together. There's not time to pull out a rosary. Heaven's going to be sick of me by the time we clear for action.

25

MAYA

Our luck lasts only a few more minutes. Both Tara and I press back against the wall as Damir turns his attention to us. He saunters over, stopping a sparse foot away.

He lifts his hand, and I almost flinch. But it's not a knife. It's a copper-inlaid bracelet. Tara inhales softly beside me.

"That was a smart move. Ditching the heartbond dampener when you realized they weren't agents." Damir twists the bracelet in his hand. "But Dejan's not so smart."

Usually hearing the news that someone has a heartbond is reason to party and start daydreaming about it happening to you. Except when in a warehouse with a psychopathic elf out for vengeance and one half of a heartbond sitting captive next to you.

Damir tosses the bracelet away and another muted sound escapes Tara.

"He's still got his on. Or did," Damir amends. "But he felt some of the panic earlier. Should we take off the iron and let him feel something again?"

I don't know what I'm going to do as the insanely stupid part of me urges me to lunge in front of Tara as Damir moves.

Damir laughs, teeth flashing bright in a smile that's too wide. He strikes quicker than a snake. One moment, I'm braced in front of Tara. The next, I'm on my side, blinding pain bursting across my cheek and temple. My sobbing gasp is broken by a boot crashing into my stomach. I curl up, somewhere between almost vomiting and desperately searching for breath.

"Leave her alone!" Tara shouts. Dampness tracks hot paths down my cheeks, blurring the tableau of Damir hauling a struggling and fighting Tara up by her arm.

"No..." I push an elbow against the ground, fight still thrumming somewhere inside.

Damir stops, head whipping around seconds before a rippling *boom* trembles through the ground, dislodging dust from above. He shouts, but brilliant blue and intense *heat* throws the side door off its hinges, blowing it halfway across the warehouse.

And all hell breaks loose.

26

DEJAN

ROSSER AND CREW THREE arrive with bare whispers of sound. One moment it's empty alley behind us, the next it's like they're just *there*.

"That agent was dirty?" Rosser asks, voice low.

Cieran nods. Rosser's face twists in anger.

"Sorry," he tells Besim, who just nods tightly.

Energy hums through me, my magic rushing through my veins. For the first time in a long time, I wish I had combat magic like Rem. My friend seems to sense this and knocks his fist against my shoulder. There's a little warning, and a bigger promise in his look. He's got my back, and he's going to do everything to get Tara and Maya back.

"Rem's clocked signatures of six hostiles inside," Cieran updates. "There's another five on the perimeter. Two hostages inside. Possibly some deep cover agents too."

Ylan was with Damir yesterday. Good chance he's in there now with no way to let us know other than a code word and his own wily strategy.

"Plan?" Rosser asks. Our chances are significantly better now with their team which includes two casters, and with Crew Seven two hundred yards away behind another warehouse building.

"You're hitting the front door. We need a distraction."

Rosser smiles thinly and glances at Seb. The red-haired half-fae tilts his chin up. The expression is almost gleeful on him.

"Seven's running exterior and establishing perimeter. Remy's not clocking much warding on that main door, so you guys should be able to get in quick and meet us. We're breaching east side through the smaller door."

"Sure that's smart?" Rosser flicks a glance at Besim, accompanying me in that look. He got the full brief somewhere in transit. He knows I've got someone I care about—and someone I want dead—inside.

Cieran huffs. "They're gonna try and go in anyway. Might as well be where I can see them. All the same, get your asses in there."

Rosser jerks a sharp nod, falling to adjusting the bracers on his forearms.

"Good?" Cieran asks and gets wordless affirmations in nods or thumbs-up as rustles marking weapons and comms check go around.

Cieran gives Seven the go-ahead through comms to move up on the west side with the screen of parked semitrucks. Three has the straightest path to the main doors visible from here. Cieran waves his hand and we move, splitting east and threading around a line of brick office buildings.

I'm third in line. My spot for the last five years. My bow stays holstered and my hand closes around my sword hilt.

Fates, I could use some of Besim's faith right about now. He's been back to rock solid since we got back in the truck and he started silently praying. Cieran glances around the corner and signals. We follow, boots whispering soundlessly over the dirt and weed-cracked concrete between buildings.

"Set," Rosser reports.

"Set," reports Crew Seven.

Cieran checks with us one more time. Remy steps forward, deep blue magic wicking around his wrists. The sharp scent of his magic floods the alley along with an increase in temperature.

Cieran nods. "Go."

Remy waits until Seb hits the front with reverberating power before thrusting his hand forward at the door. It doesn't stand a chance. Cieran's moving, shield raised and broadsword up before it's done being blown off its hinges.

He and Remy split to the left, and I veer right, stalling at the sight of Damir twenty feet away holding Tara by one arm. She meets my eyes, mouth dropping open. Then she yanks backward as hard as she can. Damir's too distracted to keep firm hold of her.

And when I shout, "Damir!" he focuses on me instead. I charge, throwing a coiling burst of stinging magic at him and driving him away from both women.

His hand flicks forward and I barely dodge out of the knife's path. He pulls another and charges, undeterred by my sword. Damir twists around my strike, his knife sticking in my tac vest as he gets close.

I drive an elbow down into his back, but he hooks an arm around my leg and lifts. We go down. My sword clatters from my hand as he lands on top of me. I throw a left hook, knocking him off-balance, enough for me to push into a roll, coming up on top.

The entire front of the warehouse shakes again, the door creaking ominously. Purple magic snakes through the air, yanking a container from the bottom of a pile. The rest starts to wobble and fall toward...I pause. Cieran and Remy are in the path, until Remy pushes Cieran and they dive out of the way.

Damir shouts something in old Slavic elvish and I'm thrown sideways, skidding across the floor. He comes back at me, and I scramble toward my feet, barely making it to my knees before he tackles me again.

I'm pinned, his knife hovering above my throat. A snarl contorts his face as he throws his full weight against me. My arms shake and my magic flares around my hands, bolstering my resistance against him. I shout, trying to force him off me.

He's suddenly gone, the crisp scent of Remy's magic trailing in his wake. A quick check to my left shows the warlock with arm still extended. He moves right into crossing blades with a fae, basalt blade sparking blue as they fight steel on steel.

Damir shouts again, shaking free of Remy's spell as two men hustle toward him. I charge again, my own knife pulled. But I've never been the best at knife-fighting, especially not against Damir. I'm only barely staying even with him, trading strikes with blades or bursts of magic to attack or block against spells. Cieran's at my side, taking on one of the men who tries to intervene. Cries behind me mark what I hope is Besim covering the women as they get out of the building.

Another *boom* hits the front. Where the *hell* is Crew Three?

———

Maya

I lurch back against the wall, away from the heat and chaos. Tara scrambles back beside me, horror on her face at the sight of Dejan fighting his cousin, sparks of green magic flaring around them. A clash of steel practically in my ear sends my cuffed hands raising like I can cast any defensive spell. It's my turn to watch in terror as Besim fights off a human almost as tall as he is.

"Maya!" Tara's panic has me twisting to her. My hands clench to fists, ready to punch as Emmet crashes to a knee in front of me.

"May, it's okay!" He spreads his hands, but I don't know that I can believe him. I jerk away as he reaches for me. "It's okay!" he reassures again, sticking a key into the cuffs. The iron falls away from my wrists with a rush of relief. He does the same for Tara.

"Get out of here." He looks between us, and focuses on me with a look so like Dad I almost want to cry. "I'm sorry." Then he's gone, running back over to Damir.

"Maya!" My name from a deeper voice has me scrambling up to my feet. Besim keeps his bloody sword angled away as he reaches behind himself with stoneskin-covered hand. I lurch against his back, almost cursing the tac vest and chain mail for the slight barrier between us. His arm wraps around me as he keeps himself between me and the fighting.

"You okay?" he asks over his shoulder.

"Yes." My voice shakes, but somewhere my mind tells me that he can't just stay here and hug me. As if he hears, he releases me.

"Get out the side door," he orders. He's already looking to the rest of his team.

I help Tara up, both of us practically clinging to each other as fights rage all over. Magic flares and snaps. She's the one who starts to nudge me toward the door as Besim fights off two more figures. One's a magic user, and I'm paralyzed again as Besim dodges spells or pushes in close to stop his opponent from being able to cast. He moves faster than I'd thought possible.

Motion in my periphery materializes into Cason. The agent has a frantic look on his face as he dodges a rogue blast of magic. He's heading for the side door. Something rises in me. He'll get away, maybe pretend he didn't have anything to do with this. Or maybe just disappear and keep trying to sell secrets.

I thrust my hand out, sending a poorly controlled version of the *push* spell at him. He throws up a hand, a warding bracelet on his wrist glowing bright green as it blocks my spell. It was enough to throw him off course for a moment. Cason bares a savage looking smile at me, then starts running. My heart falls until I see the stocky figure blocking the door.

Cason pulls to a halt. "Move!" he urges like he's talking to a friend. The New Jersey warlock only smiles thinly.

Understanding dawns across Cason's face. "You're—" But he doesn't finish. The warlock scoops his hand and slashes in a low line. Crisp wind kicks up, sweeping the agent's feet out from under him. Cason hits the ground, and his ward bracelet blocks a direct hit of the warlock's magic but it still sends him skidding across the ground a few feet. The warlock crosses the distance in two strides, grabs the bracelet, and the pulse of a *shattering* cast hits me in the face. Another spell and Cason slumps to the ground, unconscious.

The warlock turns on us and even though I know who he is, I still throw my hands out like I can protect Tara behind me. He just offers a muted version of the cocky smile he'd had in the *Fox* before he slides out the side door.

Besim's taken care of the two men somehow, and after another look at us and the empty space around us, sprints to Cieran's side. The sergeant is a whirlwind with sword and shield, absorbing magic against the shield, but I can see the rune-warded surface starting to smoke from across the warehouse.

The feeling of fae magic draws my attention to where Emmet is starting to cast a gate circle. Tara screams Dejan's name. And raw, wildfire magic *erupts*.

———

Dejan

Two men tag up on Cieran. Damir swipes at me, pushing me away from Cir's flank. Frustration clenches my jaw as I'm pushed back and back.

Damir backpedals as Remy fires another blast of magic. A black half-fae appears at Damir's side, sending a blast of vibrant grey power at Remy. I track the path, seeing Remy braced against it, his basalt blade parallel in front of him, the inlay gleaming orange as it channels his magic and counters.

Impact jars my chest and I stumble back a step, momentarily confused by the acrid smoke coiling. It explodes, wending around me and pulling me to the ground, arms pinned. Damir pounces, knife to my throat.

"Go!" he shouts over his shoulder. Two men are at his side, the half-fae raising his hands. The ground warms underneath me. I start to struggle. He's creating a gate circle that will transport us out of here.

Damir's attention whips up and he throws his knife. Remy's strangled cry shreds through me. He's on one knee, staring in muted horror at the knife stuck *through* his right forearm above the wrist. The basalt blade clatters to the ground. Pain contorts his face.

"Hex blade charmed for piercing armor," Damir calls.

Shit! It's mirrored on Remy's face. Any time he moves, the knife will inch closer to his heart. He can't pull it with the hex active or it'll jump right back into his body.

"Keep going," Damir snarls at the half-fae who'd paused.

Dread slams into me at the change in Remy's face. He's focused on his arm and the blood seeping through his chain mail and dripping to the floor. Resolve tightens around his mouth.

"Remy, don't." It's a frantic whisper.

He lifts his head to look at me. Lurches to his feet. Summons magic.

Damir curses in frustrated disbelief. The human pulls the pin from a wild magic grenade and throws it.

Remy's focus whips toward it. He's already moving. Barely flinching as he throws a containing spell over the grenade. It explodes in the shelter of the spell, wild magic coiling and smashing against the shield.

His attention falls back to us as the gate spell starts to activate, shimmering in my periphery, heat building. The same stupid stubbornness slants across Remy's face as he staggers a step forward, already lifting his free hand.

"REMY, *DON'T*," I scream, fighting against Damir and the trap ensnaring me.

But Remy keeps moving, arms moving, hitting his chest, fists clenching. He slams a foot down and a line of blue fire races toward us. I turn my face away like that'll save me, but it doesn't hit me.

I can feel it pass under me, slicing through the trap. Singeing Damir. He falls back, cursing and shouting. Remy advances, smashing fist against his chest and stomping again. His magic pours out in a wave, forcing its way over the fae magic, shoving the gate spell *apart*.

The half-fae cries out, collapsing to his knees. I lunge, tackling Damir back down, pinning him with a spell my father taught me years ago. But I miss the human and his other grenade.

I'm not the only one shouting. Cieran's on his knees, shield braced in front of him.

Remy catches the grenade in a spell as it hits the ground.

"REMY!"

My hold on my spell falters. He has to stop. Blood pours from his arm, the knife's path through his arm unhindered by the magic. Besim's trying to get to us, but he, too, appears blasted back by some force.

It's Remy.

The gate's disrupted, the half-fae clutching burned hands. Damir slams something to my chest and speaks a word. I'm thrown away from him, my head hitting hard against the concrete.

He staggers to his feet, yanking another hoarded spell talisman from around his neck. He shouts in Gaelic and throws the pendant down. Black-tinted magic starts to billow around Damir and the two others.

Until Remy grits out words in Hawaiian, each accompanied by more motions, summoning, centering more power. The wild magic from the contained grenade absorbs into his new spell. His feet brace wide, hands outstretched, calling the mixed power to him.

Damir and the others are nearly obscured. I'm just at the outskirts of whatever spell Damir is brewing. Giving me a clear view of Remy.

Fiery blue wicks off his skin, deepening around his eyes and obscuring them. Heat builds and builds, searing at my skin. His mouth is moving, but I can't hear.

"Rem," I whisper helplessly. He's not going to stop.

His magic streams out around him, blazing hotter than a forest fire. For a moment, it almost looks like fire-laced wings before he slams hands together and channels the magic right at Damir.

I twist, arm up to protect myself from the raw power. Screams barely make it over the sound.

The sorcerer spell is cleaved right in half, the smoke obliterated. The half-fae is thrown sideways. The human is not so lucky, dying almost instantly. Damir has a knife in hand, some attached counter-spell trying to redirect the oncoming fire. I see the moment it fails, the bitterness and futile anger in his face before Remy's power slashes through him.

The magic vanishes. It's eerily quiet.

A thud marks Remy going to one knee. And he *crumples*.

"*No!*" I scream. It echoes through the warehouse, chasing me to his side.

I know before I get there. Know before I touch him. I do anyway, and curse again and again.

He's cold.

27

Dejan

Blood's everywhere, pooling around his limp arm. The blade has ripped over half his forearm, almost up to his elbow in a precise line. Carotid pulse is thready.

He's alive. Barely.

Tara crashes to her knees beside me. She barely spares me a glance, searching for Remy's pulse like I did.

"Tare." I reach out and brush her cheek, pulling away when I leave bloody marks.

Her fingers squeeze around my wrist. "I'm okay," she whispers, and turns back to Remy.

"Don't." I stay her hand as she reaches for the blade. "It's a hex."

Confusion is her response.

"I need to break the hex before we can pull the knife. Don't move him." My voice is raw, but steady. She nods, healing magic rising around her hands, ready when I tell her.

I turn my attention to the knife, setting shaking hands against the hilt and cuing up my magic. Hexes are usually placed at the hilt, spinning like little machines, tracking movement and pushing the knife along. With my magic tuned for healing, this always takes time. What I need is for Remy to do this.

The thought focuses me, and I send out threads of magic, trying to locate the weak spot in the hex. It spins faster in response. I close my eyes, relentlessly searching until I find the waver in the pattern. I target it with a burst of magic. The hex spasms to a halt and fades.

"Okay," I say thickly. Tara puts her hand on Remy's upper arm. He's not moving. Not responding.

"It's sitting right against the ulnar artery. Careful," Tara says.

I curse in reply.

She closes her eyes. "Tilt it to the right. *My right,*" she hastily corrects.

I obey, moving the blade slightly.

"Okay." She looks to me, walling off emotion and nodding. "Pull it."

I slide it out. Not even a twitch from Remy.

Tara's magic swells. "I've built up around the artery, but it's—"

Bad. I don't need her to tell me that. The chain mail has been split on both sides of his arm. The knife must have hit between the bones.

I call up my magic again. I clamp my hands around his forearm, squeezing like that will help knit things back together as my magic weaves through the wound.

Only Tara's hold on my arm stops me from pouring everything I have into the injury.

"Dej, he needs a hospital." Her voice shakes. Tears well in her eyes.

Our hands and sleeves are covered in Remy's blood. I twist to see Cieran on his feet, watching. Waiting for an ambulance will take too long. Even taking the truck isn't good enough. The hospital is all the way across town.

"I can gate him." Crew Seven's earth-based warlock stands next to us. Behind him is Besim and Maya. She's clinging to his arm, staring at the semi-conscious half-fae a few feet away.

"Do it." Cieran's words are tight, barely harnessing his own panic at Remy's unconscious form. "Novak, you and Maya go with him."

I want to protest, but we've got a mess to clean up here and Tare and Maya will be a lot safer at the hospital. They both need to get checked anyway.

I grab Tara's hand. She holds me just as tight, her other hand gripping my shirt sleeve. A tremor rocks her jaw, but she manages a faint smile for me.

"You're okay?" I ask. She nods, but her hand gripping mine tells a different story.

"Dej." Cieran touches my shoulder. They're going *now*. Tara releases me and I find Remy's pulse one more time to reassure myself that he's still alive. My hands leave streaks of blood against his armor.

"You *firren* asshole," I whisper. "What were you thinking?"

But he doesn't answer. Cieran has to pull me to my feet and I stumble out of the way. Maya kneels by Tara where she's wrapped hands around Remy's arm. Tara looks at me, her "I love you," reduced to the movement of her lips in the whirl that's a transport gate forming and whisking them away.

I stare at my shaking hands for a silent moment before a half dozen expletives in elvish and common rip from me. I whirl toward what's left of Damir like I can exact any sort of revenge. Not even seeing his smoking body brings any sort of relief.

He's dead. Can't come after Tara, or me, again. But he might have killed Remy.

"Cieran." A soft drawl yanks my attention to the dark-haired elf standing just to the side. He's covered in smoke and dirt. He must have been outside.

Cieran must reply, since Ylan goes to Damir, crouches, and reaches into a vest pocket to pull out a flash drive. Tendrils of smoke surround it. Ylan smiles grimly.

"Takes care of that." He rises smoothly to his feet, pocketing the drive as he does. The other deep cover agents whose identities were on that drive are safe now. Remy has always been good at frying electronics.

My hands clench tighter. Ylan crosses over and taps my shoulder. He doesn't say anything. I don't want words anyway. Then he's gone, out into the sunlight and the rest of his mission.

Crew Three has two prisoners. Agent Cason is still alive, passed out on the floor close to the side entrance. He's cuffed and Besim drags him over to the others.

It's hours too long before everything's sorted, the men and Cason loaded up to be processed and placed securely behind bars. Captain Wolfe comes out, taking reports without a change in expression.

The only crack in his mask is when he finally dismisses us and we're free to go to the hospital and find Remy.

28

Dejan

It's only after we get to the hospital that I realize I still have blood on my hands. But there's nothing but single-minded focus among us as we're directed down to the ICU. Once there, Cieran heads right for the nurse's station.

She circles the desk before he says anything, wordlessly beckoning us to follow. Guess we should be grateful we're the only bloody soldiers to come into the ICU looking for their crewmate today.

The rooms are smaller, front walls made of glass for the doctors and nurses to more easily keep tabs on the critical patients. I did one rotation in an ICU during paramedic training. I might have ended up a nurse here in another go around. A curtain is halfway drawn over the main window, the sliding door open instead.

Cieran's first because suddenly, I'm frozen to the ground. I can't go in. Remy's only here because it's bad.

What if...?

Besim's hand on my shoulder anchors me back to the door in front of me and not the thousands of potentials spiraling in my head. I slowly step in, attention going first to Tara. She and Maya sit in chairs shoved against the far wall, out of the way of the bed and the blocky equipment.

Tara gives a small nod, reassuring. I'm frozen again. Unable to go to her, ask and make sure she really is okay. She just looks to the bed, wordlessly telling me to check on my brother.

Remy lies there, unconscious, heavily bandaged right arm resting atop the thick woven blanket. A monitor is clipped to his left index finger, blood pressure cuff circles his upper arm. IV lines run to poles set at the head of the bed, a blood transfusion halfway done. Heart monitor wires trail from under the pale blue hospital gown. Worst is the endotracheal tube running from his mouth and connecting to another machine and monitor. Air hisses, machines beep, his chest rises and falls, but he doesn't move.

I look almost desperately to the screens. Blood pressure and heart rate are low but not fluctuating. Respiratory rate is slow. The last line on the main monitor is nonexistent. It marks magic readout, and there's nothing even registering.

Shit, Rem.

A knock on the door announces an elven doctor. He introduces himself as Dr. Pedoski and sticks hands in his white coat pockets.

"What's...?" Cieran can't even get the question out.

The blond elf smiles calmly. "He's unconscious, and I'm assuming you all know how he sustained the injuries."

I don't want him to get to the bad part.

"He's intubated to protect his airway. He coded once on the operating table." Pedoski's voice is calm, even. He gives updates like these every day. "He's stable for now. However"—he points to the last readout—"his magic is gone. He used everything."

"Shit." Cieran swallows hard.

Pedoski inclines his head. "We knit his arm as much as we could, but in this case, we don't usually put much magic in when there's an absence of natural magic in a patient."

My chest squeezes. "Did I put too much in?" I ask like I'm some rookie first time on a truck or a mission.

Pedoski gives an encouraging smile. "No, you probably saved him from bleeding out before he got here. We didn't put much more in."

"His magic..." Cieran starts, stops, then tries again through clenched jaw. "Prognosis?"

Pedoski hesitates for a telling second. "The first twenty-four to forty-eight hours are the most critical. If inherent magic starts to regenerate, it's usually then."

Cieran and Bes catch what I already know.

"If?" Besim's voice has the same dangerously even meter.

I start to hate Pedoski's smile. There's nothing behind it this time. "We're hoping for the best. Let me know if you need anything." And then he's gone before I can tell him I need my friend to wake up.

"Dej?" Cieran doesn't take his eyes from Remy as he asks. He wants the truth. I'd want it in his place, but I don't want to give it. Don't want to speak it into this room that might be Remy's last place. Inherent magic is almost like a vital organ. Go too long without it, and the body will start to shut down.

"It's not good." My voice starts low, thick. Miserable. "It's rare anyone comes out of a coma. And it's only if they didn't completely drain their reserve and there's something to regrow."

My hands are shaking again, stinging hitting my eyes. "He's a *firren* idiot. He shouldn't have done that. He shouldn't..."

"Hey." Cieran faces me, and I look desperately back.

"He shouldn't have done that." Not for me.

Cieran's hands fall on my shoulders, and it feels like he's going to hold me up. "Go find a place to get cleaned up, Dej. He'll be…" He stops, eyes bright. He doesn't lie, and I don't want him to start bullshitting now. "We'll be here. Okay? We'll be here."

He's hurting too. I can see the sudden fragility around him. He's been the one in the bed. He's lost brothers. He doesn't know if he can do it again. He needs the same reassurance.

I push blood-caked fist against his chest. "We'll be here," I promise. Here for Remy, here for him. Cieran nods sharply, and releases me.

I slowly turn to Besim, who's just as fractured. It's the same wordless promise in his honest face. I grab his shoulder, and his hand gently settles on mine. I pull him down a little closer to my height and gently knock the side of my head against his. He taps my back and releases me to stumble out of the room.

Down the wide hall until I find a single bathroom. I use my elbow to depress the handle and shoulder the door open. My knees give out and I slide to the floor, back against the wall. Facing off with the sink and trashcan, the bits of paper towel that someone didn't bother picking up.

The door whispers open and Tara kneels on the ground next to me. Her arms circle my shoulders, tugging me close. I don't want to touch her with hands still covered in Remy's blood, but I lean against her.

Her hand presses against the side of my head, saying nothing as tears rip from me. I dimly feel her pulling off my heartbond dampener before wrapping her arm back around me. Steadiness starts shoring me up, not flinching at the tangled emotions raging and dripping down my face.

It feels like it's coming up from my toes. Remy became the brother I'd always wanted somewhere in the last five years, and I don't know what I'll do if he doesn't wake up. Tara and I don't have a telepathic connection, just a sharing of emotions. But I still almost hear her promise through the bond—*I'll be here.*

The tears finally start slowing until it's just my ragged breaths. Tara's arms stay around me, and her fingers gently combing through my hair start to settle me. I almost reach for her before pausing. She's in a loose hospital shirt. I don't want to get this one dirty too after I cried all over her shoulder.

I slowly straighten, bringing my arm up and using my upper sleeve to wipe the last traces away. She gently settles her hand against my back.

"I'm sorry." My voice wavers. "Are you okay?"

Tara softly smiles and nods. "I'm okay. Not too much the worse for wear." She gently forestalls my automatic apology again. "You're not the one kidnapping me."

A broken sound tumbles in my chest. "You sure you want to keep me around? In the week and a half since we met again, you've been kidnapped and held as hostage twice."

"And you were pretty heroic both times." She nudges me.

"Heroic, huh? And now I'm crying in a hospital bathroom." I scrub my eyes again.

She chuckles lightly, resting her forehead against mine. "This just in. Dejan Kostic has feelings."

I close my eyes, leaning against her. "Disgusting, right? I understand if we part ways here."

"Can't get rid of me this time, Dej." She brushes a kiss against my temple, and I further settle into something more solid. She slides a hand under my elbow. "Let's get you cleaned up."

I get to my feet and cross to the sink. She flips the water on, pushing it toward hot. I stick my hands under the stream, scrubbing off as much as I can before I even go for soap. Stop halfway to roll my sleeves up, tucking the blood out of sight.

Tara stays beside me, a steadying presence until finally my hands are clean. I rest my hand against her cheek, and she leans into the touch.

"Thank you," I whisper, touching my forehead to hers. Her arms slide around my neck.

"You're welcome," she murmurs back. The old me would never have let her see, or feel, this amount of emotion through the bond. Part of me still hates that she has. I've got my crew to thank for many things, but mostly just having taught me to be a better person. I'm still not great at actually saying a lot of things, but from her smile, she feels it just fine through the bond.

29

Besim

Tara follows Dejan, and Cieran sinks into her vacated chair. He pulls his hat off, hands clenching and pressing against his forehead as he leans on his knees. I'm swallowed by the same numbness that hit the second Remy collapsed in the warehouse. I've seen him do incredible things with his magic, but I've never felt or seen anything like that. I've also seen him bounce back, time after time.

And seeing him motionless, warm brown skin tinged almost grey in the lighting, just the beeping of the machines to show that he's *alive*...

Seeing the bag containing his clothes in the corner, the mail and tac vest on top of it, weapons and boots beside it all. The glint of his ident tags on top. Like he's already gone, and his locker's been cleared out.

Remy's parents aren't here. Have they been told? Bear? Everything wrenches sideways at the thought of his son seeing him like this. And Sara...

I'm usually so steady. So ready to reach for my faith. But I feel helpless here just watching the rise and fall of his chest, refusing to believe what Dejan and the doctor said. Refusing to believe he won't wake back up.

A shuddering breath comes from Cieran, then he crosses himself. About six months ago, he'd started sporadically showing up at St. John's, the place his sister went to Mass. The place my family and I go. At first,

I think to feel a little closer to Shay as days passed without her. But he's been there more and more often in the last few months, not saying anything as I slide into the back pew beside him. He's picking some things up, asking me questions occasionally.

It's good that he has some faith now, because I'm not sure what I have. Not sure that I can be there for him and Dejan, because I'm floundering just as bad.

"Besim."

I look down at Maya. Light bandages wrap her wrists, and some bits of dust still cling in her hair. Her hands are on my upper arms and my right hand comes under her elbow in response.

"You okay?" My question comes uneven, even though I'd checked and double-checked with an arm around her in the warehouse before she'd been gated here.

She nods, but the brightness in her eyes and way her lips clamp tells me the real truth. But she's not asking me for support, trying to give it to me instead. I want to tell her not to, to let me help her first. But she wraps her arms around my neck, one hand pressing to my cheek.

"What do you need?" she whispers.

My vision blurs for a precarious moment, and I rest my forehead against hers. Besides Remy waking up and being fine? This. Just this.

I take her hand and we head out of the room, down to one of the benches along the wall. I unstrap my vest and sword and lay them on the ground before wrapping an arm around her shoulders.

She turns her face into my chest, arms tucking up against her stomach, breaths coming shaky.

"It's okay," I murmur, pulling her closer.

"I was a-asking about y-you," she hitches against my shirt.

"We can both sit here and cry if it'll make you feel better," I say, only halfway joking. Odds are high that I might start at any time.

"It might." She slowly uncrosses one arm and loops it around me instead. "Thanks for coming."

"Always."

Her hold tightens. "Bes, I'm so sorry about Remy."

Moisture spills from my eyes and I struggle through a breath.

"And I..."

"Hey." I gently rub her arm. "It's not your fault."

"My brother was the one trying to cast that gate Remy stopped." She says that like it obviously links back to her.

"Still not you."

She shakes her head, pressing her forehead more firmly against my chest. "Fine. It's not. Anyone ever tell you it's annoying when you're right?" She tilts a look up.

Another wave of helpless grief hits me, and my jaw trembles for a second. "All the time."

And she lets me lean on her as the tears start coming.

30

Dejan

It's been seventy-one hours. I'm back at Remy's bedside. Besim's just outside the room, rosary slipping through his fingers. If I know him, he's praying for everyone on this floor, not just Remy. Cieran's down the hall somewhere. It's obviously hard for him to be down here because of his own memories of being half-conscious in the ICU with no team anymore.

And Remy? He's still comatose, not moving unless physical therapy comes by to make sure joint contractures and pressure sores aren't forming.

He's been extubated at least. One less medical device covering him. Pedoski declared him stable enough that they weren't worried about him going into sudden cardiac arrest or collapsing his airway. It came out sometime yesterday.

We weren't there. Meetings with Wolfe and other agents from the FBI are taking up our time that's not spent here. Cason's in custody, Maya's brother is going to testify on everything he can. Whatever's left of the Shrikes with Damir dead is going to be destroyed.

The Kostic legacy can fade into obscurity.

But none of that matters because part of my chosen family is still here in this bed. His parents have been taking turns here, the other staying with Bear. They've graciously tolerated us being here too.

Tara's been staying with Besim's family. Once his mom got enough details, she practically dragged Tara home to stay. After she hugged me. Something that got an eyebrow raise from Tara. I learned a long time ago not to try to dodge Marie Antilles. Tare's been getting along great with them.

She'll be involved in the inevitable court case too, keeping her away from her outreach program. She's waved off my apologies and spends a few hours a day on conference calls with her team still out on the border, making sure everything is fine. And she's understood, either coming with me or patiently waiting for me to come by after I've been here.

I shove hands in my fatigues pockets. Rem's parents took his clothes, we've got his armor at the base. All except his ident tags. They're sitting on the bedside table. Waiting for him.

It's been too long. I know it. Everyone knows it. If his magic was going to come back, it would have by now. But that line on the monitor remains nonexistent, a faded-out band with no readout to turn it blue.

He already looks thinner. Too much longer and they'll have to do something to get actual nutrients in him so he doesn't starve to death before the lack of magic does him in.

I shake my head. "Don't do this, Rem," I whisper. "You can't go on that wall. Not like this." I'm almost glaring at him through stinging eyes, daring him not to fade out quietly without a fight. "Not because of *him.*"

Where else would I have been? I can almost hear his answer, echoing the same thing I told him over a week ago when he was still blaming himself for the stoneheart. I'd jumped to save him without a second's hesitation. He was just returning the favor.

"Always have to one-up me, huh?" I sniff, scrubbing my thumb under my eye.

A light knock announces Sara Alder. The half-elf comes to Remy's bedside, standing opposite me. She got back into town yesterday and came right to the hospital, folded into the silent rotation of sentries.

She's still got a jacket on against the exterior chill, reddish-blonde hair pulled back in a ponytail. A satchel is slung over her shoulder. She gives me a tentative smile and turns her attention to Remy, stopping just short of placing her hand on his shoulder, then gently presses his hand instead.

Sara knows what really happened between Remy and Maeve Ballagh and has been cautious of overstepping any physical boundary he might have. It makes me like her a bit more that she's still so considerate when he can't do or say anything to tell her different.

"Any change?" she asks.

I shake my head. He's still cold despite the blankets covering him. No response to any touch or sound.

Sara nods, not taking her eyes off him. "They decided to bring Bear to see him finally."

It hits me unexpectedly hard. I know Blair's been losing his mind at home, unable to visit his dad. I still don't want him to see Remy like this, but it's not up to me.

"They asked me," Sara continues. "Asked me if I thought it was a good idea." She wavers. "Like I'm part of the family and have any say." She turns glistening eyes at me. "We haven't even had our date yet."

"Next Friday" is in five days.

"You've been part of the family since you went after Bear," I tell her.

She smiles, but it fades just as fast. "I just keep thinking...what if he doesn't wake up and what if..." Her eyes squeeze closed for a long moment. "Where does that leave me? What happens if one day, we just start to drift apart and I don't come around anymore? There's nothing tying us all together." Except Remy. The rest remains unspoken.

I don't think she realizes that just won't happen. She'd be a person who Remy loved and will always have a place in the Kalama house. Even if the worst happens. And even if someday she moves on.

"How long you willing to wait?" I ask.

Her look is filled with understanding. "As long as it takes."

"Hey, Bear." Besim's voice outside alerts us to the Kalamas' arrival.

"Hey, Uncle Bes," Blair replies. "We saw Cieran here too."

"Yeah." Besim chuckles. "Dej is in the room with your dad."

I force a smile when Blair peeks around the door, bright eyes sweeping around the room and settling on Remy. He blanches back before Rebecca Kalama appears beside him, hand on his shoulder.

Bear's in a jacket and jeans, boots like his dad, and oversized ARMY hat tucked on his head. He's creeping up on four and a half, but suddenly looking older as he takes another step into the room. Hesitates, then bolts the few feet to Sara's side.

He's not tall enough to see over the bedside railing, so Sara picks him up. Remy's parents hang back by the door. I feel like I'm intruding and shift to leave, but Rebecca comes around and pats my arm, silently telling me to stay.

"He's cold." Blair studies his dad.

"Yes, he used up all his magic, remember?" Rebecca says gently.

"I brought him some." Bear digs into his jacket pocket and produces a rock the size of his fist.

"Is that one of my basalt rocks?" Keahi rumbles from the door. Bear flashes an unrepentant smile at him before focusing back on Remy.

"It's just a rock, honey," Rebecca says. "There's no magic."

Bear's face sets into stubbornness so like Remy's in those moments in the warehouse that I have to turn away for a second.

"Can I be on the bed?" he asks, turning to Sara this time.

"Be very gentle," she tells him, lowering him in the space between Remy's left leg and the rail. Bear cautiously touches Remy's arm over the tattooed warlock marks banded around his forearm. The lower half of his magma dragon tattoo is visible under the gown sleeve. Bear probably has a marker and might try to color them if we're not careful.

A nurse interrupts, asking for Rebecca and Keahi in order to give them the daily update. They step out after one glance at Blair to make sure he's okay.

"When is he gonna wake up?" Bear asks me. He knows I'm the medic. I've put Band-Aides on him multiple times, pinky-promising that we're not telling Grandma and Grandpa about riding the tricycle off the curb with a hair-raising yell.

"I don't know," I say. I don't want to lie to him. Remy wouldn't want me to.

Blair scowls, pulling his cap down a little further to hide his blinking eyes. He clutches the rock in his hands.

"You promised, Dad." It comes quiet and almost angry. Then he takes Remy's hand and with a not very subtle look at both of us, puts the rock against Remy's palm. "It's like your sword. It has magic," he tells Remy like he's listening.

Sara and I exchange a helpless glance, not sure how to break it to him that it's just rock. The magma that formed it is long cooled and transformed, taking any fire magic with it. If it even came from a volcano that hosts a sleeping magma dragon.

A sudden inhale comes from Remy. His hand *twitches*. His head tilts slightly against the pillow. "Bear." It's barely audible, so faint I might have imagined it except for the hope in Sara's face.

"*Dad*!" Bear huddles against Remy's chest. Sara puts a hand on Bear, ready to pull him away if needed.

And the monitor beeps. It's faint. Trace. A slender line of blue appears at the bottom of the monitor, wavers. And holds on.

I lean over the rail, setting fingers against Remy's carotid pulse. Check the monitor. It's a few beats per minute faster than it was seconds ago.

"He's warmer," I tell her.

"Look!" She rotates Remy's left hand up. Where a chunk of rock was, a pile of broken pieces and fine dust remains.

We stare at each other in shock, confusion, almost paralyzing hope.

"Wait..." She pauses, looks at Blair pressed against Remy. "Dejan, what if...what if Blair's not a conduit for fae magic. What if he's a conduit for *Remy's* magic?"

I stare at her, barely daring to keep hoping. "Get the doctor."

31

Cieran

I hate hospitals. Almost dying in one, and then having to watch your sister die in another section of the same building will do that to you. I can barely stand to be here. Especially in the ICU ward. It could be the same room as Remy's that I spent a week and a half in over two years ago, before getting moved to a different floor once I stabilized and they did the prosthetic surgery on my right leg.

The leg in question bobs up and down. My hands are clenched together. I've only been able to do max an hour around Rem's actual room before I have to come out of the high-risk ward and onto a bench in another hallway away from the constant beeps and hiss of ventilators and sudden flurries of action of a patient coding or another trauma being brought in to settle for however long they can hold on.

I hate having to leave for bursts of time. But every time I do, Dej and Bes just silently check on me. Hell, even the Kalamas are making sure I'm okay and it's their son in the bed. I have one of Shay's rosaries in my chest pocket. I haven't actually prayed one yet, but it feels more like moral support to have a little piece of her here with me.

A few months ago, I started finally believing that there was something *more* beyond life being a string of shitty things happening. And right now I'm holding on to that as tight as I can in a way that's the easiest and hardest thing I've ever done. It makes me think that my sister's still looking out for me. Maybe even looking out for Marko since I got a text from Dave Sheridan two nights ago saying the elf had showed up at their house.

Athina's comforting presence settles beside me, and she scoops one of my twining hands into hers. She came back with Alder yesterday. Despite the argument still sitting between us, she's been right at my side as I wrestle with the possibility of losing someone again. I didn't think I'd get this close with Crew Six. Didn't think I'd let them, or myself, form more steel-like bonds with each other. Not after my old crew died.

But they're family now. Have been for months. They effortlessly folded me in, baggage and all, put their trust in me. And Remy? Rem sometimes feels like the little brother I lost years ago.

So I don't know if I can sit here and watch a sibling slowly die again.

"Cir," Athina says softly, and wraps her arm around my shoulders like she might have felt that last bit through our bond. I lean against her for a moment before moving so her arm comes free and I take her hand instead.

It's been the minutes of somehow oppressive silence in a hospital that never stills that I've finally been able to articulate what it is that made me balk over a week ago.

"I'm sorry." I owe an apology first. She tilts her head and regards me.

We don't have our heartbond dampeners on, but I've been keeping a tighter lock on my emotions and thoughts, not wanting the entire mess to spill over to her. I ease up a little, letting some more through and tapping into the bright steadiness that's her on the other side.

"It's just when you started talking about moving here and getting married, I..." I take a breath. "I just started thinking about everyone who wouldn't be there." Grief that feels ever-fresh hits again. "Shay's a year next month, and she would have loved helping you plan..." Fates. I try to scrub my eyes, but the tears have already snuck out. "And Javi won't be my best man, and..."

Athina leans against me. "Cieran, I'm sorry."

"And my parents...they died when I was twelve. It was a car crash, but my dad..." I lift a shoulder. "What if we have kids and something happens to me, and they grow up without a parent?"

She tugs me close and presses her forehead against mine. *"That's many fears to borrow from the future."* She's sometimes more comfortable in the mindspeak.

"I know," I reply in kind. "I'm sorry," I whisper. "I'm tired of feeling crushed like a rock any time I think I'm making forward progress with..." I gesture at myself.

"It is not your fault," she says. "I'm too blunt sometimes. I can push without truly thinking. I didn't even consider..."

I shake my head. "I couldn't put it into words really until..." I tilt my head toward the ICU entrance down the hall.

"How is he?" she asks quietly.

"No change." My hands go back to clenching each other until she rescues one. "But..." I take a breath. "I still don't want to just assume you're coming here. You worked so hard to get where you are in the fleets. I don't think you should just give that up without us talking about it."

She shakes her head, then stops and gives a faintly rueful smile. "You are right. But I always knew if I found an equal in a mate"—she ignores my automatic grimace at the term—"I would leave the fleets. I would apply for discharge if I became pregnant, so why force you to leave your position until then?"

"What about your family?" I press.

"You're the more important part of my family now," she says gently, pressing a kiss to my cheek. "But we will still visit Kirnae if I move here."

I chuckle slightly. That's a no-brainer.

"Cieran, you are good at what you do. You've found purpose again with Crew Six," she says, leaning against me briefly. I can't deny it. "I don't want to take that from you."

The faint fear that something might happen to me still clings to my mind. "If we have kids..." That part doesn't seem as frightening as what I'm about to say. "Maybe I should discharge. Find something safer to do."

"What would you want to do?" she asks, not trying to persuade me one way or another.

I shrug. I'd told her once that the military had been my life, had given me family and taken family away. Even with all the heartbreak, thinking about a life away from that just feels...wrong.

"Then you stay." Her steadiness wraps around me. "We can talk about it again in the future if we need to. I'm at peace with discharging from the fleets. I just want to be in a place *with* you and not leagues and leagues apart."

Her frustration with the long-distance relationship we've found ourselves in over the last year is understood and matched by mine. Fate, or more likely God, sent our paths crossing months ago in the Wastelands, and I honestly don't know what I would have done without her.

"You sure?" I ask one more time.

"Only if you can forgive me for being a little thoughtless."

I give her a flat look and she crooks a smile. This is the first time we've been out of sync about anything. I'm just halfway desperate to get back in step with her. Her chuckle lets me know she feels the thought and agrees.

"So how about it, Athina Spera? We getting married?" I ask.

She shakes her head, smile spreading across her face, brightening her copper-flecked eyes. "Can we have pie at the wedding?"

"You know I'm already in love with you, right? You don't have to bribe me." I lean closer. She just laughs as she kisses me.

There's still going to be some hard days ahead, but I'm ready to make a *home* with her.

"Cir!" Bes almost skids into the hallway. I jolt halfway to my feet, bracing for the worst. Pause at the relieved smile on his face. "Rem's waking up."

32

DEJAN

Pedoski doesn't want to believe it. It sounds like the miracle it is, but he can't deny the monitor. The way Remy's hand twitches in response to pinprick stimulus. And the way I know he feels trace magic when he scans Rem with his elf magic.

Blair still huddles against his dad, refusing to move. Keahi and Rebecca hold each other at the foot of the bed. Besim's at the door, the same painful hope in his face as he looks to me and then back to Remy. His hand slides into his pocket, likely finding that rosary again.

The doctor pushes one hand against his chin. "The magic is male dominant in your family?" he clarifies with Keahi.

Remy's dad affirms. Their magic has been passed male to male for generations.

"And Blair?" Pedoski points to him. He notices the hesitation.

"Genetic mutation," Sara speaks up. "He doesn't have it, but it's like he can sense things about Remy's and Keahi's magic. He says it makes him feel cozy when they use it." She glances around as if asking us to confirm.

"Can I?" Pedoski gestures to Blair again. The Kalamas give permission and Pedoski lightly touches Blair's shoulder. "Hey, kiddo. Can I check you real quick?"

Blair pushes up, glancing to his grandparents and Sara for confirmation. Pedoski gently takes his hand, pressing fingers against the radial pulse at his wrist. Finding a pulse is the easiest way to assess magic or injury.

"What's the rock you brought?" the doctor asks.

"It's basalt. It has magic like Dad and Grampa." Blair squirms a little.

"How do you know?"

"Sometimes it tingles like when Dad uses magic."

"It does?" Keahi asks, head tilted. He's the one with magic and it's clear he's never felt that around the rock.

"Yeah." Bear shrugs like this should be obvious. "That's why I picked that one."

Pedoski withdraws and Bear remains sitting tall, still nestled by his dad, one small hand almost protectively settled on Remy's tattooed forearm.

"Genetic mutation?" Pedoski crosses his arms, looking at the Kalamas and then at Sara like *they* were the ones who did something. "*That* is not natural."

I don't know what he discovered about Bear that the regular pediatrician hadn't noticed. But then, he was probably looking for something specific.

"His birth mother was fae," Keahi spits like a curse. "She did something to him and stole the magic."

Pedoski nods, thankfully not pressing the issue. Not asking why Blair doesn't look half-fae with pointed ears and a band of fae color around his iris. Why he's not humming with both fae and warlock magic.

"It's not stolen. It's..." His hands move, tapping each other as he tries to find the word. "Altered. Instead of him being able to pull from inherent magic, it's…" His hands stack again. "It's like the natural pathways are smoothed and hollowed out. He could, theoretically, channel some magic from something into something, or someone, else."

"So he could have helped Remy pull whatever residual is in that rock?" I ask. Bear'd been touching the rock and Remy when it happened, I'm sure of it.

Pedoski nods. "From what I can tell, it was trace amounts in the basalt. I'm not really sure what would happen if he used a more direct source."

"Is that enough to help Remy's magic regrow?" Keahi asks.

Pedoski checks the monitor. As he does, the line dims, falters, and gamely hangs on. "No. I'm afraid that if we leave him like this, the risk of him coding again and regressing goes up. His body is trying to hold on to it. But it might not be able to, and the shock of losing magic again, however small, might fully…shut him down." He doesn't say kill. Not with Blair right there.

"We can get more. Grampa has more rocks at home," Blair says.

Pedoski offers him a smile, then turns to Rebecca and Keahi. "I don't know what putting more magic in would do. This is…theoretical…and frankly, impossible."

Magic can't be transmitted back into someone. Once it's gone, it's gone.

"But again, theoretically, your magic and Remy's magic would be identical at its core."

"Bear could transmit my magic into him?" Keahi asks.

Pedoski nods. "It would have to be incredibly controlled. And I don't know what it would do to either the child or to Remy. It's a risk, and I don't know that I advise it."

A battle rages over the Kalamas' faces, and I have to turn away as I see the acceptance of losing their son return. I grip the railing. Sara presses Remy's shoulder. We'd make the same choice.

We want Remy back, but not if it risks Bear. Remy wouldn't want that either.

"I can do it," Blair says. He looks around, and when he finds refusal in his family's face, he hones onto me. "I'm not scared of the magic. Dad's never scared. I'm not either."

"Bear." My throat tries to lock up. "Your dad wouldn't want you to. You could get hurt."

He shakes his head. Stubborn. Maeve Ballagh might have tried to alter him into something else in utero, but he's Remy's kid through and through.

"We can get another rock," he insists. Then he whirls. "Grampa, we can use your pen!"

Keahi slides a hand into his pocket and pulls out a slender cylinder of polished basalt. A perfect channeling tool for a professor and renowned botanist. "What if I put some magic in this?" he asks the doctor.

Pedoski regards him. "It would have to be a small amount to reduce risk to everyone. If you're going through with this, I want a crash team on standby."

They look at *me*. Like I'm the one who can give the go-ahead on this. Like I know more than the doctor who's got multiple specializations based on the letters embroidered after his name on his white coat.

"It would have to be a small amount," I agree, my almost miserable gaze falling to Remy again. "But not if it risks Bear. He'd have to be touching the source."

"I can do it." Blair sounds so sure. But he's four and just as desperate to get his dad back.

"We'll have a crash team ready to go," Pedoski says. I'm not really sure if he's advocating for or against trying.

Keahi sighs, eyes squeezing shut. When he opens them, tears bead his lashes. He murmurs something in Hawaiian, and Rebecca leans into his shoulder.

"A small amount won't hurt Blair?" he clarifies. Pedoski affirms.

Even if it helps bring Remy back, who knows what'll happen to his magic. Pedoski steps into the hallway and calmly alerts the nurse to get a team on standby. Besim backs out of the door, making space for the team of nurses assembling in the hall to charge through if they need.

Blue wicks around Keahi's fingers where he holds the pen. It's a shade lighter than Remy's inherent magic, but he doesn't use his as often as his son does.

The basalt doesn't look much different as Keahi carefully hands it to Blair. The kid cups it in his hands, then grins and looks at his grandfather.

"The fireworks!" His eyes sparkle. Keahi startles slightly that Bear was maybe able to tell what magic he put in.

Bear takes Remy's hand again and tucks the cylinder against his palm. Nothing happens.

Fear strikes that it won't work. That the rock was just a random happenstance.

Then Remy sucks in a deep breath, almost like he's coming up from being held underwater. Motion stirs through him. Pedoski has fingers on Remy's carotid pulse and an eye on the monitor. The line thickens with each almost pained breath from Remy.

The doctor drops an elvish curse, but he doesn't call for the team. "Put a little more in," he tells Keahi.

Keahi obeys, touching the pen, channeling more magic from the tips of his fingers into the basalt. It gleams red for a moment. Bear doesn't flinch, but a delighted grin spreads over his face.

"Cozy," he whispers.

"Stop!" Pedoski orders, focusing back on Remy.

Remy draws in another rasping breath, fingers closing around the pen and Bear's hand. He turns his head against the pillow, face creasing. Then he opens his eyes.

I stagger back a step, bone-crushing relief collapsing over me.

Bear flings himself back against Remy's chest. Remy winces, confusion in his bleary look around. Rebecca starts crying and Keahi's nearly there. Pedoski releases Remy's shoulder with a smile and a nod, and ushers Sara back to take his place before leaving.

"Hey." Remy's hoarse word sends Rebecca further into tears. Keahi wraps his hand around Remy's arm, pressing the other against Remy's forehead like he's just a kid. Motion stirs at the door, but it's not nurses or doctors. It's Cieran and Besim, breathless and hopeful.

Keahi releases and Remy turns his attention to Bear sobbing against his chest.

"Hey, Bear." He winces as he tries to move, but can't. Sara's there, bringing his left arm up to settle around his son. A sleepy smile swerves across his face at the sight of her and his fingers curl around hers. "Did I miss it?" he murmurs.

I can't help but smile, especially as she leans closer. "No," she reassures him. "I would have waited anyway."

"Good." Remy's eyes shutter closed. I think he's fallen asleep, until he rouses himself with an effort. "Dej?"

Sara looks across the bed at me, and I step closer as Remy tilts toward me. I shake my head.

"You're a *firren shilsa*," I tell him, hoping Bear's not really hearing the "outlaw" words for use later.

Remy huffs, another drooping smile appearing. "Everyone okay?" He labors a little over the words.

"Yeah." I glance toward Cieran and Besim. "Everyone's good." Remy tracks toward them. Even though he's the one in the hospital bed, the same pained relief is in his face at the sight of them.

I lean down and tap the side of my head against his. "Don't *ever* do that again."

He smiles sleepily and tilts his head back toward Bear. His eyes close, and he keeps hold of Bear and Sara as he falls asleep. And the line on the monitor doesn't falter, just keeps growing.

33

REMY

It's been five days since I woke up. I moved to a room on an upper floor three days ago. Bear keeps bringing basalt chunks any time he comes, leaving them like tiny offerings. "Just in case," he says. I haven't really had the energy to process through what they told me about him channeling magic *into* me. All I know is my magic is back, and it keeps growing, somehow feeling stronger than it did before.

I'm still spending a lot of time asleep, or getting relentlessly bullied into getting up and walking short distances by physical therapy. Occupational therapy is by too, making me work my right hand and arm. Now that I've got magic back, the doctors are using some of their magic to speed up the healing process. I'm down to a light bandage around my forearm now, and they're saying the limb will have full recovery.

I'm getting better about not falling asleep mid-conversation, but it's still happening. Everyone's been around. The crew, Mom and Dad, Sara. I've fallen asleep and woken up more than once with my arms still tucked around Bear. He's colored my tattoos over and over, and there's a growing stack of pictures on the bedside table. It's becoming something the nurses and therapists love, coming in and asking what the newest artwork is.

But right now, I'm alone in the room. The clock announces it's veering toward evening. I'd fallen asleep again for a few hours, and sometime in there my parents and Bear left. I rub my eyes and sit up enough to shove blankets away and tug sweatpants and T-shirt. The nurses are still insisting on bringing extra blankets for me, but with my magic coming back, I'm gonna overheat one of these days.

A light knock precedes Sara.

"Hey." She shyly stands in the entrance, paper bag in hand.

"Did you bring food?" I ask, stomach rumbling at what promises to be *fries*. I've had enough nutrient loaded shakes and Jello to last me a lifetime.

She laughs and steps up to the bed. "Yeah. They said you'd started having more solid food. And it's Friday." She hesitates, her hold tightening around the bag.

Friday.

"We did have a date, didn't we?" I say.

Her grin lights up her entire face, scrunching her nose. She leaves her bag in the armchair and drags the rolling table over. I scoot up in the bed, giving her room to sit and position the table between us.

She starts to unpack the food. "I wasn't sure if you'd even like this. It's basically a fried chicken wrap. It might be too much. But it's one of my favorite places." She's rambling a little like she does when she gets nervous.

It pulls a faint smile from me. "It sounds amazing. As long as it's not Jello."

She laughs, immediately relaxing. "How are you today?"

"Better now." I snag a fry. "They're talking about letting me go home in a few days to go sleep in my own bed."

"Not that I don't love visiting you in the hospital, but there's cookies at your house."

I chuckle. "You don't even care about me, is that how it is?"

She ducks her head slightly, a bit of red touching her cheeks as she laughs. "I told you from the beginning, I'm only in it for the double chocolate cookies."

I take a fry from her grease-stained paper bag in retribution. "I did promise to set you up for life, didn't I?" I meant to say it lightly, but it has the hint of a deeper promise within. I never thought I'd look for anyone after what happened five years ago. But Sara busted through my wards with barely a care. She probably doesn't even realize what she's done for me beyond just helping save my son three months ago.

She's someone safe to be around. Someone I can trust. Someone I'm not scared to be myself with. The way she's steadily returning my look, I think she might understand a little.

"Hey," I start, hesitating. I know the answer, but it's something I want to ask, make sure, since I don't want to leave anything unsaid. "I know you've been around, it's just...I've got Bear, and it feels like a big ask with a kid already in the mix."

She already knows about my past baggage. In fact, she shot my baggage with an arrow after it kidnapped Blair.

Sara takes my hand, giving a reassuring squeeze. "Bear's a really great kid, and I love spending time with him. And even if for some crazy reason I didn't, he's part of your world. So that means he's also important to me."

Another rush of relief hits, with a steadier undercurrent I'm almost afraid to give a name. I thought I was in love once, but this is something so completely different. And I'm not sure how I ever thought those emotions in the past were real.

"Is that a yes to a second date?" I ask. "As long as I don't fall asleep in the middle of this one?"

Sara laughs, and the sound stirs that same heady mix of happiness and want. "What are we doing on this second date?"

"Maybe what I'd wanted to do tonight," I start. "Hawaiian barbecue, ice cream. Pistachio, obviously."

She props elbows on the table, unbothered by its slight wobble. "As long as I can get chocolate because I'm not a complete heathen. And then?"

I lean a little closer. "And then I'd ask if I can kiss you."

She closes the distance. "On the second date?" There's mock surprise belied by the smile around her eyes.

"Well, you know how fast I move," I say. She laughs, and then nudges the table out of the way. My heart thuds a little faster as she almost shyly scoots closer.

"I think I'd say yes," she replies. And even though she's a bare space away again, she waits for me to make the first move. The first kiss is gentle, tentative. Then her arms are around my neck and I'm holding her closer as each touch of our lips feels like desperately making up for lost time.

Until she pushes a little too hard and I lose my balance. I'm not quite strong enough yet to correct it, and her eyes go wide as she realizes I'm falling backward onto the bed. I'm laughing as I hit the pillow. She came with me, trying to stop herself from landing directly on my chest. She frantically tries to apologize at first, then gives up. Her laugh joins mine and she rests her head on my shoulder.

After a blissful moment, she props herself on one arm to look down at me. "Are you okay?"

"Just realizing that dating you might be dangerous." I shake my head. She rolls her eyes and kisses me again. My hand brushes the side of her face, skimming the pointed edge of her ear.

But suddenly she tears away, pushing up, something like horror in her eyes. "Sorry, I didn't mean...I'm not trying to..." She yanks back so her hands aren't braced on either side of me. Making sure I'm free to move.

"I know," I reassure, reaching for her hand.

Her shoulders slump in relief. "You'd tell me, right? If I'm overstepping?"

"I would," I tell her. That's something else for me to figure out, but I'm not nervous to with her.

She bites at her lip, her thumb brushing against my hand. "I hope this isn't overstepping or moving too fast, but ever since seeing you in a coma, and maybe losing my chance...I just...I think I love you, Remy."

It feels like I can't quite contain my smile. "That's good. Because I'm pretty sure I'm in love with you."

"Really?" she says like she can't quite believe it. I tug at her hand, and she slowly lowers to rest against my chest again. I wrap my arms around her.

"Really," I whisper.

She sighs contentedly, her hand coming to rest over my forearm. A new warmth settles in next to my magic as we lie there in silence.

Her stomach abruptly rumbling sends her face against my chest as we both laugh. She does have to help me sit back up and pulls the table back over.

I don't end up eating much. She finishes off my fries with no remorse and stays until the nurse regretfully informs her that visiting hours are done. One last kiss turns into two or three more, before she finally stands up and grabs her bag.

One more kiss along with a promise to be back tomorrow. She will be. Sara Alder lives up to her promises, and I'm going to happily spend the rest of my life making sure I return that honor.

34

Maya

I pace back and forth across my apartment, debating changing for the third time. Everything's suddenly stupid. My hair, my clothes, my face.

I don't know why I'm so flustered. I've been invited to the Antilleses' house for family dinner before, but that was before Besim and I made out in the middle of the Army base. I'm still not really sure what we are, but it feels pretty close to dating.

I check myself in the full-length mirror propped against the exposed brick wall and groan again. I shouldn't have said yes to him picking me up. Waiting is making this worse.

It's been almost two weeks since the warehouse. I'm still waking up in cold sweats some nights. Once I let that slip, he told me to call him. I have twice, and we talked a lot, the clock ticking later and later into the early hours of the morning. Once we both put on an episode of *Starfall* on our respective laptops and it was a mix of our commentary to each other and the odd echo of audio over the phone and the computer in front of me.

Okay, we're dating.

At least I know his family likes me. I think I'd probably cry if Marie and Martin Antilles didn't like me. I stayed with Nadire for a few days after everything because I couldn't quite stomach going back to my apartment yet. We talked about everything while sharing a small container of ice cream between us. And she shrieked and hugged me when I admitted to kissing Besim. Followed immediately by "there's a 'no making out in front of me' rule." I absolutely agreed.

I'm about to pick something else to try when a knock sounds. For a second, it paralyzes me, until I remember Damir is dead and Emmet is in jail. It's probably Besim.

I unlock the extra bolt I added last week and swing the door to admit him. I swear there's something magic in his smile as he looks at me.

"You look great," he says.

I shift from foot to foot. It's just a button-down blouse, distressed jeans, and ankle-high boots that have seen a little too much wear on their scuffed leather.

"Really?"

"Yeah. Hey, you're wearing them again." He halfway reaches out toward my hair. I smile. The butterfly clips wiggle and tug against my curls, trying to take flight with the happiness jolting through me. I hadn't really felt like wearing them for the last two weeks, since just looking at them reminded me of family and Emmet. I've always loved them since they were Mom's, but I might love them a little more since he likes them too.

"You ready?" he asks.

"Not really," I admit.

It's not just family dinner. It's turned into a whole celebration with *everyone*. As soon as Mrs. Antilles found out that Athina and Cieran are talking wedding, that became the primary focus. Then Remy got discharged a few days ago, and he and Sara are together. They're going to come for as long as he's able to. Tara's been staying with the Antilleses, and we're planning our actual spa date. Dejan's almost a completely different elf around her. But this is going to be the first time around everyone with Besim and me together.

"Don't be nervous." Besim takes my hand after I shrug into my jacket and grab purse and keys.

"Hmm." I quirk an eyebrow at him. "Kiss for good luck?"

"Of course." He obliges, tipping me backwards for good measure. I'm still laughing as I lock up and we head downstairs to his waiting truck.

It's loud and bright when we get to the Antilleses' house. Marie meets us at the door, apron on as she wraps me in a hug and ushers me in.

"Always so good to see you, Maya. Get her coat, Besim."

He shakes his head, hanging both our coats on the rack by the door. We make our way into the main kitchen and dining area. Remy's sitting at the table, still a little pale, almost trying to fend Marie off as she makes sure he has anything he could possibly want.

Drinks are shoved into our hands as greetings are passed around, as well as some obligatory teasing from his siblings. Then Martin claps his hands, and a blessing is prayed, and food starts being served at the hand-crafted table.

For a second, among all the food and laughter and stories, I almost feel like crying. I haven't been a part of anything like this in years. Had almost given up on finding it, or feeling this *wholeness* again.

Emmet's asked to see me, but I haven't responded yet. I'll probably go eventually, and I know Besim will support me if, and when, I do. I slip my hand into his under the table and he squeezes gently.

Then we're all moved outside to the wide patio with lights strung across the pergola, two firepits warding off the evening chill as more drinks and desert are served. Slowly the Antilles clan peels off until it's just me beside Besim, one hand warmly laced in his. Dejan's arm is around Tara as they sit on a cushioned bench to our right. Athina's legs are tucked up on their seat, leaning against Cieran. Remy and Sara have the fourth side of the fire.

It's another hour of more laughter as all four of them swap stupid stories about each other. I wipe tears away as Dejan protests, "I did *not!*"

"I have photographic evidence." Besim's laugh is rapidly becoming one of my favorite sounds in the world.

"I have to see this now," Tara says.

"Later, when he's not here and can try to delete it," Besim tells her. Dejan scowls but there's a smile not far underneath.

Remy and Sara are first to leave. Despite the laughter, he's been yawning and blinking heavily for the last few minutes.

"Take care of him, Alder," Dejan says as they stand and say goodbyes.

"I will," she replies. Remy just bumps fists with Dejan, and nods to Tara. Dejan watches them leave, slightly braced until Remy makes his slow way inside and a burst of sound marks them saying goodbye to the remaining Antilleses.

Cieran and Athina aren't far behind. She slides an arm around him as they stand.

"Tomorrow?" she asks Tara.

The elf nods. "I'll text you. I have to ditch my clingy boyfriend after he takes me to lunch."

Dejan rolls his eyes as Athina flashes a smile. "Maya." She turns to me. "We are shopping if you want to come."

I shake my head regretfully. "I have class all day tomorrow. I've missed too many days recently and tests are coming up so I shouldn't skip."

And I need to get back to regular rotations at the *Fox* so my budget can accommodate something like clothes shopping.

Both she and Tara are disappointed. "Spa day soon, though," Tara says. "We're going to make Sara take a day off. She works too hard."

"Pot and kettle, my love," Dejan tells her and gets an elbow to the ribs.

Athina flashes another smile. "She is good for you," she tells Dejan.

The elf gives a small, but perhaps the most genuine smile I've ever seen on him. "I know," he says.

Tara blushes and Dejan just tugs her a little closer. Cieran moves, dropping a hand on Besim's shoulder as they pass. Besim taps his hand with a fist. Dejan lifts his chin in the same wordless communication.

Tara sighs and tips her head against Dejan's shoulder. "Come on, you can walk me upstairs."

He lets her pull him to his feet, and he and Besim bump fists as they pass. And then it's just us sitting together.

I rest my head against the back of the wicker sofa we'd claimed. The stars wink, smaller pinpricks around the gentle golden lights swaying in the light night breeze. I don't know if I really believe in fate. Besim would probably call it something more like divine providence. But whatever it is, I'm giving a silent *thank you* for bringing me here.

"You ready to go home?" he asks. For a moment, I wish that home is a place he'd already be and not a quiet apartment.

"Not really," I admit. He chuckles and lightly kisses my forehead. I want to finish my degree. I know he'd encourage me to before we take any step bigger than dating. I shift so I'm leaning against him and his arm is around my shoulders.

For the first time in awhile it feels like life is finally unstuck. Like I can take it with both hands and start living. It's the feeling that lingered around all of us as we sat here, all a little more whole beside each other.

I know one day, probably soon, he and his crew are going to leave on another mission, and the four of us women are going to band together in support. Waiting until they come back.

But right now, I'll take the quiet beside him and the way he kisses me again. The future holds a lot of uncertainty. It's never going to be perfect. But it is going to be good.

The End

What's Next?

I HAVE SEVERAL SPINOFF series planned, including the return of Sergeant Ylan Larsen and his deep cover team, but no firm release dates yet! Stay updated by following me on Instagram or by subscribing to my newsletter. Subscribers get access to newsletter exclusive short stories!

Acknowledgments

We did it. The biggest thank you for coming with me on this journey. This is the longest series I've written to date, and like any project, there are so many people to thank.

Brigitte and Jenni for beta reading and being examples of strong women and giving endless support. Gillian and Mollie for being some of the best friends ever. Deborah for being an amazing copyeditor and fangirl. My family for supporting and giving me plenty of inspiration for the Antilleses and Kalamas. And the snark between the crew.

And of course, each and every reader who's read, left reviews, or DMs/comments that made my day and made this author journey a little brighter.

Each book and series comes with challenges, doubts, fears. And this series was no exception. In fact, sometimes it felt like more than usual because it was spread across five books. Each book had its own fear attached. But somehow, this one didn't. This one gave me a few fits and starts before I finally got into it and started wrangling the plot threads together. Maybe it was finally writing Besim and Maya's story. Realizing how to tie things from Conduit off. Finishing Dejan's journey. And giving Cieran and Athina their happy ending. But this one...this one stood on its own, looked back at me, and just acknowledged that we did it.

Crew Six's stories are done. And yes, they're living happily ever after ;). Except for maybe some cameos in some future books. They taught me a lot, and I'm blessed to hear how they've helped and bolstered some of you as well. I might not always remember the lessons from writing this series, but hopefully I'll always come back to them.

Write boldly. Live bravely. Cling to Faith. And Fear No Fire.

Thanks again for reading. And thanks always to God for the gifts He's given and nurtured.

See you on the flip side for more adventures. Stay courageous, friend.

~Claire

MORE BOOKS BY C.M. BANSCHBACH

The Drifter Duology

LARAMIE WAS BORN TO ride the desert wilds. And she won't let anything stop her, even a fearsome warlord who wants her captive–or dead.

A genius mechanic–and a rare descendant of the once-magical Itan–Laramie drifts from dusty town to dusty town in search of the family that was taken from her.

But her rambling desert journey becomes a game of survival when Laramie crosses a ruthless warlord's territory. Taken prisoner by one of the warlord's biker gangs, she befriends a quiet, dangerous man named Gered. After surviving hellish circumstances Gered is tired of fighting for a better life.

Laramie will always fight. And she'll stop at nothing to win their freedom.

Enjoy this pulse-pounding motorcycle adventure in a post-apocalyptic western setting with found family and being brave in brutal circumstances. Complete series available!

The Spirits' Valley Duology

A man born for war. A bastard raised in contempt. Only together can they defend their tribe from slaughter.

Fierce-hearted Comran is the chief's son and the favored choice to be the next leader. Then his father chooses Comran's half-brother Etran for the role, straining the loyalties of the tribe and reinforcing the distance between the two men. When Comran is offered the role of battlewolf, he is ready to do his duty—but expects no friendship in return.

Steady Etran has long been shunned as the chief's bastard. Becoming the chief brings even more hostility, so he offers Comran the title of battlewolf to maintain tribal unity. But can he trust this reckless warrior as his general when Comran has never stood by his side?

As tensions mount within the tribe, a traitorous act leads to war. Comran and Etran must overcome their inner demons and fight for their brotherhood before the Greywolves fall to their worst enemies.

Read now!

———

Subscribe to C.M. Banschbach's newsletter for free short stories and book/publishing updates! http://eepurl.com/gwcGjD

About C.M. Banschbach

C.M. Banschbach is a native Texan and would make an excellent hobbit if she wasn't so tall. She's an overall dork, pizza addict, and fangirl. When not writing fantasy stories packed full of adventure and snark, she works as a pediatric Physical Therapist where she happily embraces the fact that she never actually has to grow up.

She writes clean YA/MG fantasy-adventure as Claire M. Banschbach.

Facebook – https://www.facebook.com/cmbanschbach

Instagram – https://www.instagram.com/cmbanschbach/

Website – https://clairembanschbach.com/